# Sinbad's Seven Voyages

## and other stories from "The Arabian Nights"

### retold by Gladys Davidson

SCHOLASTIC INC.
New York Toronto London Auckland Sydney

No part of this publication may be reproduced in whole or in part, or stored in a retrieval system, or transmitted in any form or by any means, electronic, mechanical, photocopying, recording, or otherwise, without written permission of the publisher. For information regarding permission, write to Scholastic Inc., 730 Broadway, New York, NY 10003.

ISBN 0-590-43520-5

12 11 10 9 8 7 6 5 4 3 2 1          9/8 0 1 2 3 4/9

Printed in the U.S.A.                    01

# CONTENTS

# The Seven Voyages of Sinbad

DURING THE REIGN OF THE CALIPH HAROUN
Alraschid there lived in the city of Bagdad
a poor porter named Hinbad, who had to toil
very hard in order to earn a wretched living.

One hot summer's day he was given a heavy
burden to carry from one end of the city to
the other, and feeling very tired, upon reaching
a certain quiet street, where a gentle breeze
was blowing and rose water was sprinkled on
the pavement, he sat down to rest for a while
against the walls of a great house.

A grand feast was going on within, and the
merry sounds of a concert of music soon
reached the ears of the porter, and wishing to
know to whom the house belonged, he went up
to a slave who stood at the gate and asked the
name of his master.

"What!" cried the slave, "you live in Bagdad, and yet don't know that this is the house
of the famous Sinbad the Sailor, who has
traveled all over the world!"

Now Hinbad had often heard of this Sinbad, who was one of the richest men in Bag-

dad, and feeling envious of the great sailor, as he compared his good fortune with his own wretchedness, he could not help crying out aloud:

"Oh, what a difference between happy Sinbad and wretched Hinbad! I have to toil hard every day, and can scarcely earn bread for my family; but he has all that money can buy, and lives a life of constant pleasure! What has Sinbad done to deserve such happiness, and what have I done that I should remain so wretched?"

In saying this, he stamped the ground with his foot, as if he had given up everything in despair.

Now this complaint was heard by those within the house, and presently a slave came out to take Hinbad before his master.

It may easily be imagined that Hinbad was, indeed, very much surprised at the compliment that was paid him. After the words that he had used, he began to fear that Sinbad had sent for him so that he could punish him, and therefore he tried to excuse himself from going, saying that he could not leave his load in the middle of the street; but the servant, assuring him that it would be taken care of, pressed him so much to go that the porter could no longer refuse.

He was led into the great hall of the house, where a splendid feast was being held and a large number of gaily dressed guests were sitting round a table covered with rich dishes.

At one end of the table sat a pleasant-looking man, whose long white beard showed that

5

he was getting on in years, and round about him stood a number of slaves ready to carry out his commands. This was the famous Sinbad, the giver of the feast; and still fearing that his hasty words had offended the great sailor, Hinbad trembled as he humbly paid his respects to him and to the rest of the company.

However, he need have had no fear, for Sinbad received him very kindly, and made him sit down at his right hand and enjoy the feast. When the astonished porter had made a good meal, Sinbad said to him:

"You are welcome here and your day is blessed. Tell me, what is your name and what trade do you follow?"

"I am called Hinbad, my lord, and I am but a poor porter who carries upon his head merchants' goods for hire."

The master of the house smiled at him and replied, "And I am called Sinbad of the Sea. Know, O Hinbad, that my story is a truly wonderful one, for I came to possess this grand palace and this great wealth only after I had toiled much and had suffered many perils. I have made seven voyages and connected with each is a marvelous tale. Listen, and I shall tell you my story."

## THE FIRST VOYAGE OF SINBAD

My father, a very rich merchant of Bagdad, died when I was only a child. He left me a great fortune which, when I was old enough to take over, I heedlessly spent on rich living, thinking always that my wealth would last forever. When at last I came to my senses, I found to my dismay that I had spent almost every penny my father had left me. So I decided to sell what little remained and use the money to buy goods and all that I would need to become a merchant. I then embarked on a ship with a group of other tradesmen and traveled to many different cities and towns, where we sold and exchanged our wares.

One day we came upon a most beautiful island, and the captain cast anchor so that we might land. Some of us decided to walk about, while others made fires for cooking, or sat talking, or eating, or drinking. Suddenly we heard the captain shouting, "Run for your lives! Run to the ship! This is not an island, but a huge fish!" And it was so. The fish had been lying there for so many years that the sand had settled upon its back. Trees had taken root and grown upon it so that it seemed indeed to be an island. Now the warmth of our fires had caused the fish to stir.

All of us ran hurriedly for the ship. However, not everyone could reach it before the fish plunged deep into the water. Fortunately Allah preserved me from drowning and sent my way a huge wooden tub that had been tossed from the ship. By sitting in the tub and paddling my feet I was able to keep afloat. But I was not able to catch up with our vessel before it sailed away and out of sight. All that night and the next day I was tossed by the wind and waves until at last I reached the shores of an island. Flinging myself down on

7

the ground, I slept like a dead man until the sun awakened me the next morning. To satisfy my hunger and thirst I found island fruits to eat and sweet spring water to drink, and after a few days I began to recover.

I decided to explore the island, and as I was walking about I chanced to see in the distance some kind of strange creature standing near the shore. Upon coming closer I found it to be a most wonderful mare, tied with a rope to the ground. The mare cried out, and, at the same time, a man came forth from under the earth and asked, "Who are you and why are you here?" I told him how I had almost drowned and how, thanks to Allah, I had been carried safely to this island. He in turn told me that he was one of King Mihrjan's groomsmen. Each month the groomsmen would bring to the shore all of the royal mares that had not yet foaled. They would leave the mares there to attract the sea stallions. The grooms would hide underground so that they would not frighten the creatures away.

The groom then introduced me to his companions, and soon we all set out for the palace so that I might visit their king. King Mihrjan welcomed me cordially, and when I had told him my story, he said, "My son, you have been most miraculously saved. Let us praise Allah for His goodness."

His Highness treated me most kindly and made me his harbor master in charge of all incoming and outgoing vessels. I served King Mihrjan a great while and learned many new and wonderful things about the people of other lands. But although I liked serving as a harbor master, I had a great longing to see my home again. I tirelessly asked visiting merchants and seamen if they knew anything of Bagdad, and it saddened me greatly to learn they knew nothing of it at all.

This sadness stayed with me until one day I went in to the king and found with him a group of Indians. We talked of our countries and I was amazed to learn that the Indian people are divided into 72 castes, some being called Shakirijah, who are the noblest class and who never fight; and others being called Brahmans, a folk who never drink wine, but delight in caring for camels, horses, and cattle. I also saw, in King Mihrjan's lands, an island called Kasil, which I visited out of curiosity since a mystic sound of drums was to be heard there every night; and on the way to this island I saw fish from sixty to a hundred and twenty yards long, and other fish that had heads like owls.

King Mihrjan's capital lay on the seacoast, and had a splendid harbor, where ships arrived every day from all parts of the world; and one morning, as I stood watching the unloading of some bales from a newly arrived vessel, I saw, to my surprise, that these goods were marked with my own name.

I then went on board, and found that the captain was indeed the one with whom I had set sail. He was delighted to see me again, and to know that I had escaped drowning after all;

and I soon made up my mind to return home with him.

I took a handsome present from my bales to King Mihrjan, telling him how I had met with my merchant friend again; and, after thanking him for his kindness to me, I bade him farewell.

The king was much pleased with my present, and also made me a more valuable gift in return; and then having taken on board a quantity of precious woods and spices, I set sail once more.

We passed several islands, where we sold or exchanged our goods, and at last we arrived in Balsora, where I landed with the fine sum of a hundred thousand sequins.

I hurried on to Bagdad; and, having bought a splendid house, I gave money away to the poor, and settled down to enjoy my good fortune.

Sinbad stopped his story here, and, sending for a purse of a hundred sequins, he gave it to Hinbad, and invited him to come to another feast next day, when he should hear more of his adventures. The delighted porter hurried home to tell the good news to his family, and next day he returned at the same time to Sinbad's house, dressed in his best clothes. Another feast was being held; and as soon as Hinbad and the other guests had finished, Sinbad began the story of his second voyage.

THE SECOND VOYAGE OF SINBAD
I had determined, after my first voyage, to

10

pass the rest of my days in peace and quietness at Bagdad. But I soon grew tired of my idle life, and desirous of seeing foreign countries, I went to sea again with another party of merchants.

We did a brisk trade from island to island, and soon added greatly to our fortunes.

One day we landed on a desert island to refresh ourselves with the delicious fruits we saw there, and as I afterwards felt rather tired, I lay down alone in a quiet spot to sleep. When I awoke I found to my horror that the ship had sailed without me, and that I was left alone upon a desert island, with no chance of escaping from it, since it was not a place where ships were likely to call.

At first I was full of despair at my sad lot; but after a while, knowing that sighs were of no avail, I began to look about me.

I soon noticed a huge white object lying at a little distance, and making my way towards it, I found that it was a dome as smooth as polished ivory, and at least fifty paces round. I walked round to see whether there was an opening, but I could find none. I tried to climb it, but only slipped back each time; and as I stood gazing upon it, I noticed that the sky was suddenly growing dark, as though covered with a dense black cloud.

I soon saw, to my astonishment, that this blackness was caused by a monstrous bird flying down toward me. I had often heard sailors speak of a giant bird called a roc; and I made up my mind that this terrible creature flying toward me was one, and that the great white dome beside me was its egg.

Seeing in this monster a means of escape for me, I crept as closely as I could get to the white dome, so that when the giant bird a-lighted and sat on her egg, she covered me also with her great wings. I then tied myself firmly with my turban to one of her legs, which was as thick as the trunk of a tree, and when she arose next morning into the sky she carried me away with her.

When she had risen to a great height she came down so suddenly that I fainted; but when she reached the ground I recovered and unfastened myself at once. I had only just set myself free when the roc, having snatched up in her bill an enormous serpent to serve her as a worm, flew away.

I found that I had been left in a very deep valley, surrounded on every side by such vast rocky mountains that it was impossible to climb them, and so I was no better off than before. As I walked along this valley I found that it was strewn with diamonds of the largest and most dazzling kind, and since I had nothing better to do I filled all my pockets and loose clothing with them.

I also saw a swarm of dreadful serpents, a sight which filled me with terror. These serpents were so long and large that the smallest of them was huge enough to have easily swallowed an elephant. To my relief, I found that they remained in their dens throughout the day to hide from the roc, and only came out at night.

I wandered about all day in this beautiful valley of diamonds, and when night came I crept into a cave and blocked up the opening with stones, that I might be safe from the terrible serpents, which I soon heard swarming and hissing outside.

Gazing about as I began to settle myself within the cave, I suddenly grew sick with fright. For there, at the upper end of the cave, was a huge serpent asleep as she sat on her eggs. I committed myself to fate and spent the night sleeplessly watching. When dawn finally came, I cautiously removed the stones and hurried away from that awful cave. Tired, filled with fear, and hungry, I began to walk about the valley.

Then a strange and mysterious thing happened. There fell from the sky to the ground before me a slaughtered animal. Marveling at this, for there was no one around, I remembered what traders and travelers had told of the perils and terrors in the mountains of the diamonds. Because of these terrors, the diamond merchants devised a clever means of obtaining the stones without risking their lives.

They took sheep, slaughtered them, and cast the cut up pieces of meat into the valley. Because this meat was sticky with blood, some of the diamonds clung to it. At midday, the hungry eagles and vultures swooped down upon the meat and carried it off to the mountaintops. The merchants, who had been hiding there up to this time, came out and shouted at the birds to frighten them away. Then they gathered up the diamonds. And this was the only way that these precious gems could be obtained.

Just as I was thinking these things, another piece of meat fell, and at once it occurred to me how I might escape from the valley. Unrolling my turban, I used it to tie myself to the meat. Thus hiding myself completely, I lay on my back and waited. Soon an eagle swooped down to seize this very meat and carried it off, with me hanging on, to a mountaintop. The bird had scarcely begun to eat when there was heard the noise of shouting and wood clattering. Frightened, the eagle flew away, and I released myself from the meat.

The merchant who had just shouted came out from his hiding place and went up to the meat to look for the diamonds. Finding none therein, he cried out, "Alas, alas, the pity of it! There is no majesty or might save in Allah. How has this come to be?" He had not yet spoken to me directly, because, I think, he feared me.

I told him then, in a friendly manner, who I was and how I had come to be in the mountains of the diamonds. I told him of my travels and of the marvelous things that had happened to me. Giving him some of the gems, I said, "I have diamonds sufficient for us both. Be of good cheer and fear nothing."

The man rejoiced, and thanked and blessed me. As we talked, the other merchants came to hear my story, and hearing it, they said, "Praise be to Allah for your safety, for no one has ever reached yonder valley and come out alive."

We passed the night in a safe place, and the next day we journeyed over the mountains until we reached a fair island. There I sold some of the diamonds for gold and silver coins, and also traded some for goods. I journeyed with my merchant friends from town to town and valley to valley, till finally, coming to Balsora, I left the merchants and returned to Bagdad.

At home once more I rejoiced with my relations and friends and gave them many gifts and presents. Now that I had so much wealth I made merry and tried to forget all my sufferings by taking pleasure in all the delights of life. Many came to ask me about my adventures in foreign countries, and they wondered at my story and gave me joy for my safe return.

All the company marveled at the story which Sinbad had just told to them. The feast continued, and the master ordered that 100 dinars of gold be given to Hinbad, who thanked and blessed the generous seaman.

The next morning, after praying the dawn prayer, Hinbad hurried back to the palace. When the guests had all arrived and the wine was flowing freely, Sinbad signaled for silence and said, "Listen then, my brothers, for my next tale is even more wondrous than those you have already heard." And Sinbad began the story of his third voyage.

The happy life that I had spent since my last voyage had made me forget all the dangers I had gone through, but as I was young and strong I again got tired of my lazy life.

It was not long therefore before I set sail once again with another party of merchants, to seek adventures and treasures. We made a long voyage, trading at the various places we came to; but one day we were caught in a terrible storm, which drove us out of our way.

We drifted along for some days; and then as the storm continued, we were obliged to enter the harbor of a certain island, where the captain was very unwilling to take shelter. He told us that in all the islands about here there were hosts of wild savages, who, although but dwarfs, would soon overcome us, and if we dared to kill but one of them, they would destroy us all; and what he said proved only too true.

Presently a swarm of the most frightful savages came swimming towards us and clambered into the ship. They were covered with red hair, and though the largest was not more than two feet in height, they were so fierce, and came in such vast numbers, that we could not keep them back. We dared not harm them, and in a very short time they unfurled the sails, cut the cable from the anchor, and made us get on shore. They then hauled our ship away to another island, from which they had come.

We soon found out that the island where we had been left was a very dangerous one and was always avoided by all ships that passed that way, for a reason which I will tell you presently.

We left the shore and walked into the island a little way, where we found some fruits and herbs, which we ate, and soon came to a huge palace, larger than any we had ever seen before. We entered through the gateway and found ourselves in a large hall, on the one side of which, to our horror, was a great heap of human bones, and on the other a number of spits for roasting.

While we were trembling at this fearful sight, there suddenly came into the room a most horrible giant, who was as tall as a palm tree, and had but one great eye like a red burning coal. This eye stood in the middle of his forehead. His long sharp teeth projected from his mouth like tusks, his ears hung down over his shoulders, his nails were long and curved like the talons of a huge bird, and he was altogether such a dreadful-looking monster that we all lost our senses at the sight of him, and lay on the floor like dead men.

When we opened our eyes once more, the ogre was still looking at us; but presently he seized the captain, who was the fattest of our number, and holding him in his hand as though he were a sparrow, he thrust a spit through him. He then made a great fire, and roasted and ate him for his supper, and when he had finished he lay down and fell asleep,

17

his snoring sounding like the rolling of thunder. Next morning when he awoke, he went out and left us alone.

You can imagine the terror we were all in; indeed our fear was so great that at first we were powerless to think out a plan of escape. We spent the day wandering about the island in search of fruits and herbs for food; and when night came we were forced to return to the palace, since we could find no other place of shelter. The ogre soon appeared, and having again supped upon another of our companions, he lay down and slept until morning, when he arose and left us.

This went on for several days; but at last I suggested that we should try to make some rafts and escape by sea. We found plenty of wood about the shore, and when the rafts were ready we returned to the palace for the last time.

The ogre came as usual, and having eaten another of our party for his supper, lay down and fell asleep; but this time we found courage to take revenge on him. Each one of us that were left seized spits, and making them red hot in the fire, we thrust them all at once into the giant's great eye and blinded him. He sprang up with a terrific yell and rushed out of the castle, howling with pain.

Directly he had gone, we all rushed down to the shore, and launched our rafts; but no sooner had we got on board than the ogre appeared again, with several other giants as large and dreadful as himself. We got away from the shore as quickly as possible; but the monsters came striding into the sea after us, and taking up great stones, they threw them at us with great force.

Unhappily they aimed so well that they sank all the rafts except the one on which I was seated with two others, and we were the only ones who escaped drowning.

We rowed with all our might until we got out of reach of the giants, and after being tossed about for a long while by the waves, our raft was at length thrown upon an island.

We passed the night upon the shore, but were rudely awakened by a loud noise caused by the rustling of a fearful serpent as long as a palm tree. It swallowed one of my companions, and full of terror, the two of us that were left fled away to a great distance, groaning at the dangers to which we were constantly exposed.

Next day we saw the serpent again. Though at night we climbed up into a tall tree for safety, it found us out, wriggled up the trunk, and swallowed my companion, who sat lower than I. It then went away, and next morning I came down from the tree and made a great circle of brambles and thorn bushes all around my hiding place.

I climbed back to my perch, and when evening came the serpent returned, but was not able to get through the circle of wood I had made. He crawled and hissed outside all night, and did not leave me till day. I waited a little longer, and then coming down from the tree, I rushed toward the sea, meaning to

19

throw myself in, since I could bear my troubles no longer.

Just as I was about to throw myself amidst the waves, I saw to my joy a ship not far out, and by wildly waving my hands I managed to attract the notice of the captain, who quickly sent a boat to fetch me on board. On hearing my story, the captain received me kindly, giving me food, and bidding me rest. Seeing that I was in rags, he also gave me some of his own clothes. I found that those on board were merchants, and we traded at all the places we came to.

One day the captain came to me, and putting some bales of goods into my charge, asked me to arrange the sale of them for him, saying he would pay me well for my trouble. I gladly accepted his offer, not caring to be idle among so many busy people; but great was my astonishment when I found that the bales were entered in the name of Sinbad.

Going up to the captain I now recognized him as the one with whom I had set sail on my second voyage, and upon my asking him about the man to whom the bales had belonged, he said: "They belonged to a merchant named Sinbad, who, having landed on a desert island, did not return with the others. We did not notice his absence until four hours later, and then it was not possible for us to return for him, since we were caught in a gale!"

"You think him dead then?" I asked.

"Certainly," replied the captain. I then looked at him steadily, and said: "No, captain, he is not dead; for you behold in me that same Sinbad, who was left upon the desert island!"

The captain now recognized me; and embracing me with great joy, he restored to me my bales of goods.

We sailed from island to island, buying and selling spices and precious woods, and many were the curious creatures with which we met on our way. One time we saw a tortoise about twelve yards in length and breadth; and another time I caught sight of a sea beast which was the size and shape of a camel.

At last after a long and prosperous voyage, we returned to Balsora, and I arrived in Bagdad with such great riches that I knew not their value.

When Sinbad had finished this story, he gave Hinbad another hundred sequins, and told him to come next day to feast and hear more of his adventures. The porter gladly did so, and when the feast was over, Sinbad began the story of his fourth voyage.

### THE FOURTH VOYAGE OF SINBAD

The very happy time that I spent after my third voyage did not prevent me from venturing out to sea again. So I gave way to my love of adventure, and having bought goods for trading, I went on board another merchant ship.

We had not been long at sea, however, when we were caught in a sudden gale. Our ship soon struck on a rock, and most of those on board were drowned. I, together with a few of the merchants and the sailors, managed to cling to pieces of the wreck, and after struggling with the waves for a long while, we were all drawn by the force of the current toward an island that lay before us.

Here we were soon seized by some natives, who took us to their huts and shared us among them. They made us sit down, and soon gave us a certain herb to eat. I noticed that none of the natives touched this herb themselves, so I would not take any either; but my companions, thinking only of their present hunger, ate greedily of it. I soon saw that the herb had indeed been given us for a purpose; for in a very short time my friends lost their senses, and knew not what they said or did. The natives then gave us rice cooked with cocoanut oil, but I ate only a very little of this.

I now knew that the natives were cannibals, who gave their victims an herb to deaden their senses, that they might not know the fate in store for them, and who afterwards fattened them with rice. I was glad I had refused to eat the herb, so that I still knew what I was about.

My poor companions were soon fattened and eaten by the cannibals; but seeing that I kept thin, they left me alone, and after a while I managed to escape from them.

I wandered about for eight days, when I drew near to the sea again, and presently I came across people like myself, who were gathering pepper, which was very plentiful in that part. I went up to them and was delighted to find that they understood me when I spoke to them.

I told them the story of my adventure with the cannibals, and they rejoiced with me in the escape I had had. When they had finished their pepper gathering, they took me away with them to their own island, and presented me to their king, who received me with much honor. He was greatly interested in my story, and inviting me to stay at his court, he gave orders that I should be well cared for.

I learned much from these people, but I was greatly surprised to find that they all rode their horses without saddles, bridles, or stirrups, and had never even heard of such things. With a slave to help me, I soon set to work to make a saddle, and when it was done I covered it with velvet and gold and presented it to the king, together with a bit and stirrups I had also caused to be made.

The king was delighted with his gifts, when I showed him how to make use of them; and as all his lords wished me to make such harness for them also I was kept hard at work and soon grew rich with the money they paid me for my trouble.

One day, when I went to visit the king as usual, he told me to my surprise and dismay that he had arranged a marriage for me with one of the chief ladies of his court; and as I dared not refuse the honor thus thrust upon me, I was very shortly afterwards married to this lady. My wife, however, soon became ill and died, and then I found myself in a most horrible fix.

It was the custom of that place for the living husband to be buried with the dead wife, and the living wife with the dead husband; so no sooner did my wife die than I was ordered to be buried alive with her, and though I begged hard for mercy, being a stranger, none was shown me.

The burial place of the island was a cave at the top of the mountain, and the king and all his court came to pay me the last honors.

When we arrived at the top of the pit, my dead wife, dressed in her most gorgeous robes and dazzling jewels, was lowered in an open coffin to the bottom of the cave, and then my own turn came. My tears and pleadings were all in vain, and I was quickly placed in an open coffin and lowered into the cave, together with a jug of water and seven little loaves to keep me alive a short time longer. The top of the cave was then covered over with a huge stone, and I was left to starve slowly to death.

Now I did not mean to die, if I could possibly find some means of saving my life. I slipped out of my open coffin and tried to grope my way about. But the cave was so dark I could not find any means of escape, so I returned to my coffin and ate some of my food.

I lived in this horrible place for several days, and then when I had eaten the last morsel of my bread, I prepared to die.

Just then, however, I caught the sound of something panting and moving at the other side of the cave, and full of hope, I followed this sound as well as I could in the darkness. As I drew nearer, the thing puffed and panted harder than ever, as though running away from me; but I followed it steadily for a long time, till at last I could see a light in the distance. I went on eagerly, and soon found that the light came from a hole in the rock, large enough for a man to get through. I scrambled through the hole as quickly as I could and to my great joy found myself upon the seashore. Then I discovered that the sounds which I had followed were caused by the panting of a creature that came out of the sea to prowl about the cave.

After I had rested and rejoiced at my escape, I went back to the cave and collected all the jewels and rich stuffs I could find in the coffins. Having brought these to the shore, I made them up into bales, and then waited for a ship to come by. I had not long to wait, for a merchant vessel soon came past, and hearing my cries, the captain sent a boat to fetch me. Thinking that some of the people in the ship might belong to the island I had left, I made up a story about having been shipwrecked and cast ashore with the goods they saw. The captain was ready enough to believe this story, and he took me on board at once with all my bales, even refusing to take the jewels I offered as payment.

We visited several interesting islands, where we did good trade, and after a long voyage I at last arrived safely in Bagdad.

In my thankfulness for my happy return I

gave splendid gifts to the mosques and spent large sums of money for the support of the poor, and then I once more gave myself up to enjoyment with my friends.

Sinbad stopped here, and giving the porter another purse of a hundred sequins, he invited him to come the following day and hear the story of his fifth voyage.

Hinbad did not fail to come, and when he and the other guests had feasted, Sinbad went on with his story.

## THE FIFTH VOYAGE OF SINBAD

The dangers that I had gone through did not cure me of my love of travel, and in a very short time I bought goods and went off to sea again, in a ship of my own this time, together with some merchants I had invited to go with me.

We made a long voyage, and the first place we stopped at was a desert island. Here we found a roc's egg, as large as the one I had seen on my second voyage. Seeing that it was just ready to be hatched, my companions, in spite of my warning, broke open the egg with their axes.

They then pulled the young roc out, and making a fire, they roasted and ate it.

They had hardly finished their feast when the two parent rocs appeared in the sky, and in much fear we all returned in haste to the ship and set sail. The two rocs drew near with a great noise, and seemed to be in a frightful rage when they saw that their young one was gone.

Presently we saw them flying toward us, carrying great stones, or rather rocks, in their fearful claws. They hovered just over the ship; then one of them let fall a stone that missed the ship and fell into the sea, which dashed up like a great wall of water. But unfortunately the other roc aimed better, and dropping his enormous stone into the very middle of the ship, splintered her into a thousand pieces.

I was the only one to escape drowning. After being tossed about by the waves for some time I was at last able to reach the shores of an island not far away. I found plenty of fruit to eat, and having refreshed myself I lay down and fell asleep.

When I awoke, I began to walk about the island, which had an abundance of trees and clear bright streams. There were fair scented flowers all about, and I heard the sweet warbling of birds.

Coming to a streamlet, I saw sitting there an old man, girt about the waist with a cloth made of palm leaf fibers. I thought perhaps this man too had been in the shipwreck, and like myself had made his way safely to this island. I greeted him, but he returned my greeting with signs and said not a word.

"O old sir," I asked, "why do you sit here?" He only shook his head and moaned, gesturing with his hand as if to ask me to carry him on my shoulders to the other side of the stream. Thinking that he might be an invalid, and that I might win a reward in heaven if I did carry him as he asked, I took him on my back to the spot he had pointed out to me. "Old sir, you may dismount now," I said.

But the man would not get off my shoulders. He wound his long rough legs about my neck, clinging to my throat so tightly that I almost choked. The air grew black before my eyes, and I fell senseless to the ground. But I was soon forced to get to my feet, for the old man began to beat cruelly my back and shoulders with his hard heels.

Thereafter like a captive slave I carried the old man about the island. He would gesture to me with his hand where he wished to go, and were I to refuse to do his bidding, or were I too slow-moving for him, he would fall to beating me viciously with his heels.

The old man never dismounted, either in the day or in the night. He would at times lean back, and with his legs coiled about my neck, sleep for a while; then, rising, he would beat me again and make me carry him to some fine fruit trees so that he might eat to satisfy his hunger.

Tired and suffering, I repented that day on which I had taken pity on the old man. In return for the good I had done him he had done me only evil. I swore by Allah that I would never again do any man service. I prayed that I might die and thus be released from my sufferings.

In my wanderings about the island I came upon some dry gourds; I gathered up one, scooped out its insides, and filled it with the juice squeezed from grapes. Then I stopped up the gourd and set it in the sun to permit the juice to become a strong wine. By drinking it every day I found that I could bear my hardships more easily, for the warm wine clouded my senses and cheered my heart.

One day, as I was lifting the wine gourd to my lips, the old man motioned to me as if to ask, "What is that?" I answered, "It is an excellent wine that cheers the heart and revives the spirit." So saying, I ran and danced with that fiend on my back, I clapped my hands and made merry. Seeing this, he ordered me to give him some wine. I feared to refuse him, so I yielded him the gourd. I watched him drain it of all the wine at once, and I was glad to see that it soon made him so lively and careless that he began to sing and jump about on my shoulders.

In a short time he loosened his arms from about my neck, so that I was at last able to throw him to the ground. Quickly seizing a great stone I crushed the life out of him.

Full of joy that I had managed to get rid of this tiresome old wretch, I hurried down to the beach, where I was fortunate enough to meet with some sailors who had landed to take in water for their ship. They were astonished to see me; when I had told them of my horrid adventure, they said that I had had a very narrow escape, since I had fallen into the clutches of the famous Old Man of the Sea, who never let go of his victims till he had strangled them.

They then took me to their ship, where I was well received by the captain, who was glad to hear that I had overcome the Old Man of the Sea.

We soon landed on another island, and here I began to trade in cocoanuts with some other merchants. We went to a great forest of cocoanut palms, which grew so tall that we could not possibly climb them to get at the fruit; here we saw more apes and monkeys than I had ever seen before in all my life. The merchants I had joined began to throw stones at the monkeys in the trees, and the monkeys, full of rage, pulled the cocoanuts from the branches and threw them down at us in revenge.

We gathered up the cocoanuts at once, and in this manner we were soon able to fill the great bags we had brought with us.

By going to this forest every day, and selling the cocoanuts which I got from the monkeys, I grew very rich once more; at last I was able to take a great store on board a merchant ship that called at the island. Trading at the other islands round about, I exchanged my nuts for spices, pearls, and other things of value. After doing a good trade and gaining great riches I set sail for Balsora.

When I arrived in Bagdad I made a vast sum of money by the sale of my pearls and other goods, and after having given away valuable presents to the poor according to my usual custom, I was glad to settle down to rest and pleasure once again.

Having finished this story Sinbad sent the porter away with another hundred sequins, begging him to come again on the morrow; next day, when Hinbad had enjoyed the usual feast, he began the story of his sixth voyage.

## THE SIXTH VOYAGE OF SINBAD

I had only been at home one short year when, weary of such a peaceful life, I made up my mind to go to sea once again in search of adventures. This time I went on a longer voyage than I had ever undertaken before, and we met with such stormy weather that for a long time we were driven out of our way altogether.

At last, however, the captain suddenly found out where we were. Then full of dismay and fear, he tore off his turban and cried out like a madman. We asked him why he acted in this manner, and he replied that we were caught in a most dangerous current of the sea, a current which was so terribly rapid that in less than a quarter of an hour it would carry the ship along with it and dash her against the rocks.

We found this to be but too true. The ship was being carried along at a terrific rate, and in a few minutes she was dashed to pieces at the foot of a great rocky mountain.

We managed, however, to save our lives and the greater part of our goods and food; but we soon saw that it was impossible for us ever to escape from that dreadful shore. The frightful current that had brought us along so swiftly would prevent us from sailing away, even if we had a boat, since it came with such force toward the shore that there was no fighting against it. Also the great mountain on the coast rose to such a dreadful height and was so rocky and steep that it would have been madness to attempt to climb it.

So we were completely shut in by the sea in front and the mountain at the back: We had nothing but death to look forward to.

We divided our food equally among us, and we expected to die when it was gone, since no fruit or food of any kind was to be met with in that lonely place.

I spent my time wandering about the shore and lower part of the mountain, which I found to be very rich in precious stones. Among the wrecks that had been cast up on the shore I came across handsome goods and treasures of great value.

I also noticed that a strange river of fresh water ran from the sea into a dark cave; and this I thought a great wonder, since in all other places rivers ran from the land into the sea, and not from the sea into the land.

As our small stock of food was used up my companions grew weaker and weaker and died one by one; at last I, having been more careful than they in making my portion of food last out, was the only one left. I expected soon to follow my poor friends, but one day, just as I was coming to the end of my small store, I happened to wander near the bank of the great river that flowed from the sea into the cave which I had noticed before. As I gazed at this strange river I suddenly thought that it must have an outlet somewhere. Since I could not well be any worse off, I made up my mind to build a raft and allow the current to carry me where it would.

Quick as thought I set to work, and soon built myself a strong raft with the pieces of wreckage that lay on the shore; then I loaded it with bales of rich stuffs, rubies, emeralds, and other precious stones I had found, together with the scrap of food I had left.

When all was ready I took two little oars I had made and went on board; and having guided the raft carefully into the cave I allowed the strange river to carry me along.

For several days I floated in utter darkness. Sometimes the roof of the cave was so low that it caught my head, and I had to lie flat upon the raft or I should have been killed.

At last I came to the end of my food; being very weak and weary, I soon afterwards fell into a half-fainting state and knew not what I did nor where I went.

How long this dazed state lasted I don't know; but when I once more came to my senses and opened my eyes I found myself, to my great surprise, lying in a meadow on the bank of a river, where my raft was still floating, though it was now tied to a stake. A number of natives surrounded me; but though they spoke to me I could not understand what they said.

Full of joy for my escape I uttered aloud a prayer of thankfulness in my own language;

then one of the natives, who, it seemed, understood Arabic, came and spoke to me in the same tongue. He said that he and his companions belonged to the country I was in. Having come to dig little canals from the strange river which flowed out of the great mountain close by, they had seen my raft and brought me off for safety to the shore.

The natives gave me some food, and after refreshing myself I told them of all that had happened to me. They thought my adventure so wonderful that they insisted I should go with them at once to their king to tell him my story.

So I went with them to the capital of Serendib, as the island was called. When we arrived at the royal palace the natives presented me to their king, who received me with such honor and kindness that I offered him the whole of the treasures upon my raft as a mark of my regard for him.

But this truly noble prince refused to take any of my riches, and instead, constantly added to them by handsome gifts of his own. He was so struck with my wonderful adventures that he caused an account of them to be written in letters of gold and placed in his treasure house.

He gave orders for me to be treated with the same honor and respect as were his own great lords. I was shown all the beauties and places of interest in the country, which I found to be very rich indeed in precious stones and rare plants.

When I returned from viewing the country

34

I begged the king to allow me to go back to my own land; and not only did he graciously consent, but he also made me another splendid present of even greater value than any he had given me before. He also asked me to carry from him a letter to my sovereign lord, the Caliph Haroun Alraschid, together with a most noble gift. The letter was written in azure upon the skin of an animal of great value; in it he humbly begged the caliph to accept his gift as a mark of the admiration and friendship he had for him. The present consisted of spices and aloe wood; a cup, half a foot high, made out of a single ruby, and filled with enormous pearls; a snakeskin, the scales of which were said to possess certain healing powers; and lastly, a slave-maiden of dazzling beauty, whose robes were entirely covered with glittering jewels.

I bade farewell to the king and his lords, and set sail in the fine ship that had been got ready for me, and as soon as I arrived in Bagdad I went to the royal palace and presented the caliph with the letter and the gift sent him by the King of Serendib.

The caliph received his gift with much pleasure and great surprise at its richness, and he asked me if the King of Serendib was really so rich and splendid as one would suppose.

I then gave him an account of the great magnificence of all I had seen in the island, telling him that the royal palace was covered with a hundred thousand rubies, that the king had in his treasure house twenty thousand diamond crowns, and that when he went abroad he sat on a throne fixed on the back of an elephant, with a guard of a thousand men, clad in cloth of gold and silk, going before him, mounted on a hundred elephants all richly draped.

The caliph was greatly interested to hear of this powerful king, whose riches were so wonderful, and when I had finished my story he sent me away with a handsome present.

Sinbad stopped here, and giving the porter his usual hundred sequins he invited him to come once again to hear the story of his last voyage. Hinbad and the other guests came next day at the proper time. When dinner was over Sinbad began the story of his seventh and last voyage.

### THE SEVENTH VOYAGE OF SINBAD

I was glad to settle down in peace once more to enjoy my riches; since I was now getting on in years, I made up my mind to run no more risks of danger and adventures by land and sea, but to spend the rest of my days in ease and comfort.

However, I had no sooner made up my mind to follow out this wise plan than one day the caliph sent for me to come before him at once. When I arrived at the palace the caliph told me that he wished to send a handsome gift to the King of Serendib, and he desired that I should be the bearer of it.

I explained to the caliph that I had made up my mind to go to sea no more and told him of the many terrible dangers I had gone through; but he still insisted that I should go, since it was most fitting that I, being already known to the king, should take the gift. He said that I only needed to take a letter and the gift to Serendib, and then return; so at last I agreed, and the caliph, well pleased, gave me a thousand sequins for my journey.

After a few days I went on board ship and set sail for Serendib, carrying with me the caliph's handsome gift and letter of friendly greeting. The gift consisted of many pieces of cloth of gold and of other rich stuffs; two splendid royal beds; a dish made of agate, an inch thick and half a foot wide; and a valuable tablet, said to have belonged to the great King Solomon.

I arrived safely in Serendib, and going straight to the royal palace I presented to the king the letter and gift.

The King of Serendib recognized me at once, and received me with much joy. He was quite delighted with the friendly letter and the splendid present sent him by the caliph. He wished me to stay with him some time, but I begged to be excused, being anxious to return home; so he made me another gift and allowed me to depart.

I went on board and set sail, meaning to return to Bagdad at once; but, alas! this was not to be. A few days after we got out to sea we were attacked by fierce corsairs or sea robbers; in a very short time they captured our ship and made prisoners of all on board. We were stripped of our clothes and made to put on ugly rags, and then the corsairs took us away to a strange country and sold us as slaves.

I was bought by a rich merchant, who took me to his house, dressed me in fine clothes, and treated me very kindly. Finding that I could shoot well with bow and arrow, he one day took me with him on an elephant to a thick forest some miles away from the town. Here we stopped, and putting a bow and arrows in my hand, he pointed to a tall tree, saying: "Get up into that tree, and shoot at the elephants as they come past. There are a great number of them in this forest, and if you kill any of them, come and tell me."

Giving me some food, he returned to the town, while I climbed up the tree and waited for the elephants to appear. None came near me that day, but early next morning a great herd of them came tramping past my tree. I shot my arrows into the midst of them, and at last I succeeded in killing the largest. I then returned to my master, who was very much pleased with what I had done. After I had eaten some food, we went back to the forest and buried the dead elephant, my master meaning to return later to take its ivory tusks, which were of great value.

After this I was sent every day into the forest to shoot elephants for my master; and then, one time, a very strange thing happened to me. It was about two months since I first became a slave, and I was sitting in my tree as usual, with my bow and arrows, when the herd of elephants, instead of passing by as they had always done before, came suddenly toward me with a great rush, making a dreadful noise. They quickly surrounded my tree and stood staring solemnly at me for some time; then the largest of them suddenly put his trunk round my tree, and rooting it up, threw it to the ground. I fell off, but was not hurt; then the elephant lifted me up with his trunk, and setting me on his back, began to march forward at a great rate, followed by the whole herd.

Presently he set me down on the ground again and went away with his companions; there I lay for some time, more dead than alive, as you may imagine.

Finding that the elephants did not return, I got up and began to look about me. I found myself on a hillside which was almost covered with the bones and ivory tusks of elephants, and I soon made up my mind that this must be the burying place of these strange creatures, which had evidently brought me there to show me that I should keep from harming them, since I did so only for the sake of their ivory tusks, to which I could now help myself without troubling them further.

Quickly I left the hillside and returned to the city, which I reached in a day and a half, and when I told my master of my adventure, and of the vast treasures of ivory I had so unexpectedly come across, he was full of amazement. He showed great joy at seeing me again, for having found my uprooted tree and bow and arrows, he had quite expected that I had been killed. After I had rested and refreshed myself, we took an elephant and returned to the hillside of which I had told him. Here we loaded the elephant with as many fine ivory tusks as he could carry; and on our way back to the city my master said:

"Sinbad, I shall treat you no longer as a slave, for your discovery has made me rich for life. For years the forest elephants have killed great numbers of slaves; but you have been saved from their fury, which is a sign that Heaven favors you. All the merchants in the city will be grateful to you, for they will no longer need to risk the lives of their slaves, since there is ivory enough on that hillside to make all in our city rich and powerful. Not only do I make you free, but I will also give you great riches, and the very next ship that comes into the harbor shall carry you back to your own land."

I thanked my master for his kindness, and until a ship arrived I helped him to collect ivory. As soon as a vessel came into the harbor, it was got ready for me, being loaded with ivory and other valuable goods as well as food for my voyage. When all things were set in order I bade my late master farewell, and set sail. I traded on the voyage with my ivory, bought splendid gifts for all my friends, and at last I arrived safely in Bagdad.

I went at once to the caliph and told him of my adventures, which he thought so curious that he caused an account of them to be written in golden letters for himself.

This was my last voyage. At length I was able to settle down with my vast riches in peace and comfort.

When Sinbad finished his story, he said to Hinbad: "Now, my friend, you have heard what dangers I have gone through, and do you not think that after such troubles I deserve to live a life of peace and enjoyment?"

"Ah, yes, my lord," answered the porter, humbly kissing Sinbad's hand, "your sufferings and dangers have been terrible, and my own troubles and hardships are as nothing compared with yours. You are worthy of your riches, and I trust you will live long to enjoy them."

Sinbad was so pleased with this reply that he gave Hinbad yet another hundred sequins, and said he looked upon him as one of his best friends; begging of him to give up his work as a porter, he invited him to come and feast with him every day.

So Hinbad the porter became a rich and happy man, and all the rest of his life he had good cause to remember with a grateful mind the kindness of Sinbad the Sailor.

# Aladdin
## and the Wonderful Lamp

THERE ONCE LIVED, IN A CERTAIN LARGE CITY
of China, a poor tailor named Mustapha, who
was so very badly off that though he worked
hard all day it was as much as he could do to
keep himself and his household from starving.
To make matters worse, his only child, a boy
named Aladdin, had been brought up so
badly, was so lazy, careless, and disobedient
that, instead of being a help and comfort to
his parents, he was only a trouble to them.
He was really a clever boy, but instead of
learning all the wise and useful things he
could, he chose to play about in the streets
with other idle children. Even when he grew
older, and was put to learn his father's trade,
he still refused to work: Directly he was left
to himself, he would run away to join his
wicked companions for the rest of the day.

At last the poor tailor, quite overcome by
his own misfortunes and grieved at his
son's bad conduct, became very ill and died.
The mother, finding that Aladdin did not
mean to work at his father's trade, sold up the

things in the shop, and tried to earn a wretched living by spinning cotton.

Aladdin still went on with his idle, careless ways until he was almost grown-up, and then a strange thing happened, which changed the whole course of his life for the better.

One day a stranger, who was really a wicked sorcerer, or wizard, known as the African magician, passed through the city and saw Aladdin at play with some of his idle companions. Noticing at once that the lad was really quick and clever, he made up his mind to make use of him in carrying out some secret plan which he had on hand.

So, after learning what he could about him from the bystanders, he called Aladdin to one side and asked him if he was the son of Mustapha, the tailor.

Aladdin replied that he was, but that his father had been dead a long time. Then to his surprise, the stranger threw his arms around his neck and kissed him many times, weeping as he did so. On being asked by Aladdin why he acted thus, the African magician told him that he was his uncle, and that he wept for the death of Mustapha, the tailor, who was his brother. He then gave Aladdin a handful of small money and told him to go back to his mother to tell her that his newly-found uncle would visit her the next day.

Full of surprise and delight, Aladdin ran off home at once and asked his mother if he had an uncle. The poor woman replied that he had not, and when Aladdin told her about the stranger who had just spoken to him, she decided there must be some mistake, for though her husband had certainly had a brother once upon a time, he had long since been dead.

But next day Aladdin again met with the African magician, who kissed him as before, and putting two gold pieces into his hand, told him to take them to his mother and bid her get a good supper ready, as he meant to come and see her that night without fail.

He made the lad show him the house where he lived and then went away.

In great excitement Aladdin ran to his mother. Giving her the two gold pieces, he told her what the stranger had said; this time she got ready a supper for her expected visitor, greatly wondering who he could really be.

When evening came, the African magician arrived, bringing wines and rich fruits with him for the supper. When they were all seated at the little feast, he told Aladdin's mother that he was indeed her husband's long-lost brother, whom all had believed to be dead, and that for forty years he had been traveling about in various parts of the world, until at last he had such a longing to see his brother Mustapha once again that he had returned to China only to be met with the news of his death.

Now all this was really only a wicked story, but the cunning magician wept so bitterly when he spoke of his brother's death, and declared that he felt so much love for Aladdin, because of his exact likeness to his father, that the poor widow began to believe that he

44

spoke the truth; and as for Aladdin, he was quite ready to accept for his uncle a stranger who treated him so kindly and seemed so rich and powerful.

So when the magician said that he meant to provide for Aladdin and start him in life as a rich merchant, the mother was very willing that he should do so, hoping that her idle son would now turn from his bad ways and be a comfort to her. Aladdin, though he had always hated work, was delighted at the idea of so easily becoming a rich and powerful merchant.

And now the magician, having made such a good beginning, felt well pleased with himself and soon hoped to make use of Aladdin for his own wicked purposes. On the very next day he took the boy out with him into the city, first of all buying him a handsome suit of clothes, and then taking him to all the places where the richest merchants met together. He invited many of them to a grand supper at night, which he gave in honor of his pretended nephew.

Aladdin was full of delight at the happy prospect now before him, and when the magician came again for him next day, saying that he must now visit the many splendid gardens and palaces on the borders of the city, he was only too eager to go. He gaily bid his mother farewell, little dreaming of the dreadful adventure that would befall him ere he saw her again.

The wicked magician did not mean that the poor widow should ever see her son again, for that very day he determined to carry out the plan he had formed for which he wished to make use of Aladdin.

So he took the boy to the borders of the city, where the richest people lived in fine houses and palaces set in the midst of most beautiful large gardens; and by constantly telling him of finer sights yet to come, he artfully led him through garden after garden until they were a great way from the city.

When they began to feel hungry and tired, the magician suggested that they should rest by a fountain in one of the gardens. Drawing out a handkerchief full of cakes and fruits which he had brought with him, he spread it out for a meal, and while they ate he talked very kindly to Aladdin, advising him to give up his idle ways and bad companions and to seek wise friends and useful knowledge, since he would soon be a man and have to make a name for himself.

When the meal was over they went on with their walk, leaving the gardens behind them, and going far out into the country, in search of the most beautiful garden of all, so the cunning magician said.

Aladdin had never been so far before, and he did not like the looks of the high mountains and the lonely country through which they were now treading, but the false uncle told him many interesting stories to prevent him from noticing where he was going and from feeling too tired.

At last they came to a narrow valley between two mountains; here they stopped, the magician saying they would go no farther, for he would now show Aladdin something very wonderful. He first of all bade the boy gather together some dry sticks in a heap for a fire. Then when this was done he made a great blaze, and throwing into the midst of it some incense powder, which caused a dense smoke to arise, he uttered several magical words.

Instantly the ground opened just in front of the magician, showing a large flat stone, with a brass ring fixed in the middle of it.

Aladdin was so surprised and terrified at this magic that he tried to run away; but his pretended uncle seized hold of him, and with scolding words, gave him such a rough box on the ears that he fell to the ground. The poor lad got up again with tears in his eyes and asked his uncle what he had done to deserve such treatment.

The magician now spoke gently to him again, saying that he must certainly obey him as his uncle if he wished to obtain the good things in store for him. He then told Aladdin that beneath the stone before them there was hidden a great treasure, which would be his alone if he would obey him. He also said that Aladdin was the only person in the world who was permitted to lift the stone, and that if he would seize hold of the brass ring, at the same time uttering the names of his father and his grandfather, he would be able to raise it quite easily.

Aladdin, having now got over his fright, and being full of curiosity, did exactly as his uncle told him; and when he had pulled up the stone he saw beneath it a hollow space a few feet deep, with a small door, and steps leading down into the ground.

"And now, my son," said the magician, "listen to what I have to say. Go down those steps, and through an open door, which leads into three great halls, in each of which you will find four large brass vases on either side filled with gold and silver. Be sure you do not meddle with these; above all things, do not touch the walls, even with your clothes, or you will die instantly! Go straight forward without stopping, and at the end of the third hall you will find another door leading into a garden planted with most beautiful fruit trees. Walk along the garden path until you come to five steps, at the top of which you will see a niche that holds a lighted lamp.

"Take down the lamp, put out the light, pour away the liquid within it, and then bring it to me. Do what I desire you at once; but if you wish for any of the fruit in the garden you may gather as much as you like!"

As he said these words the magician took a ring from his pocket and put it on Aladdin's finger, saying it would protect him from evil so long as he did as he had just been bidden. He again told him to go boldly down the steps and to bring back treasures that would make them both rich for life.

Aladdin was quite ready to obey, and jumping into the little cave, he went down the steps soon finding himself in the hall of which his pretended uncle had spoken.

Not taking any notice of the great vases of gold and silver on every side, he went quickly through the three halls, being very careful not to touch the walls, even with his clothes, for fear he should die. When he came to the garden, he walked along the path until he reached the five steps, at the top of which he saw an old lamp burning in a niche.

He took it down, put out the light, emptied the liquid, and hid the lamp safely in his clothes. He then took a good look at the garden, in which he found trees laden with the largest and most beautiful fruits he had ever seen, some of which were white, some clear as crystal, and others red, green, blue, purple, or yellow.

Now these fruits were really diamonds, rubies, pearls, emeralds, sapphires, and other precious stones. But Aladdin, having no idea of their great value, thought they were made only of colored glass; yet, being pleased with their beauty, he thought he might as well take some of them home with him. So he quickly filled all his pockets and the two new purses his uncle had given him, and even stuffed his loose clothes quite full of the pretty fruits; then, loaded with riches, of the value of which he had no idea, he returned through the three halls with great care, and ran up the steps to the mouth of the little cave.

The magician, full of impatience, called down through the small opening for Aladdin to hand him up the lamp first of all, since it would be in his way as he scrambled through the hole; but Aladdin said the lamp did not trouble him, and he would give it up when he came above ground, if his uncle would lend him a hand to help him out of the hole.

This made the magician angry, and he said he must have the lamp first before he helped him out; but Aladdin, having filled his clothes so full of the fruits, could not well get at it, and still refused to give it up until he got above ground.

The magician now flew into a most violent rage. Throwing some more incense into the fire above, he again uttered some magic words, which caused the stone to move back to its place on the top of the cave, and the ground to cover it over as before, so that poor Aladdin was thus buried alive.

This cruel act served to prove that this pretended uncle was no real relation of Aladdin, but as wicked a magician as any in the world. For a great number of years he had lived in Africa, that country of mystery and of wonders, where he had learnt all the magic and evil enchantments he could. Having found out that there was in the world a certain wonderful lamp, which, if he could only obtain it, would make him richer and more powerful than any king in the world, he made up his mind not to rest until he found it. By his enchantments he had lately learnt that the magic lamp lay hidden in a strange underground garden in a certain part of China, in exactly the place just described; so he had set off at once to the city which was nearest the great treasure that he wished to obtain.

Now although he knew exactly where the lamp was, the magician learnt from his books that he was not allowed to take it himself, nor even to enter the underground garden, but that he must receive it from the hands of someone else. It was for this reason he had made friends with Aladdin, thinking that he was a lazy lad whose life was of no value, and meaning, when he had got the lamp from his hands, to bury him alive in the cave, that he might tell no tales.

However, the magician's own foolish impatience and hasty rage had spoilt his fine plans, and feeling that his hopes of obtaining the wonderful lamp were now gone forever, since he had not the power to open the ground again, he quickly started back for Africa that same day. He was full of disappointment because he had failed to obtain his great wish, but he felt that at any rate Aladdin would not live to tell the story of what had happened, and this unkind thought comforted him a little.

However, there was one thing the bad magician had forgotten. This was the magic ring he had placed on Aladdin's finger, which was now the means of saving the poor lad's life, as we shall see.

When Aladdin found himself shut up in the cave in complete darkness, and knew that he was buried alive, he was full of dismay and surprise, for he had never expected that his pretended uncle, after treating him so kindly, would play him such a cruel trick. He called out that he was now ready to give up the lamp if his uncle would open the ground once more. But his cries were all in vain, since they could not be heard by anyone; so the poor boy could do nothing but lie on the steps and weep in despair.

For two days he remained like this. Then feeling that he would soon die, he clasped his hands together to pray for the last time. By joining his hands he rubbed the ring given him by the magician, not knowing of the magic power it possessed.

But no sooner had he thus rubbed the ring than instantly there rose out of the ground before him an enormous genie, who said to him: "What wouldst thou have with me? I am ready to obey thee as thy slave, and the slave of all who possess the ring upon thy finger — I and the other slaves of the ring!"

At almost any other time the sight of a genie would have frightened Aladdin so much that he would have been unable to speak; but now the horror of being buried alive overcame all other fears. He answered at once: "Whoever you are, get me out of this place, if you can."

Directly he had spoken these words, the earth opened and closed again, and he found himself alone in the open air once more, just in the very place where the magician had made the fire.

As soon as Aladdin had got over his surprise, he made up his mind to try to find his way home again. Although he had been brought so far out into the country by the magician, who he now knew could not have been his uncle, he was glad to find that he remembered quite well how they had come. Having once made his way into the gardens, he soon reached the city, and went straight to his home.

Want of food, and joy at being safe home again, completely overcame poor Aladdin; but as soon as he was better and had taken a little food, he told his mother of all the dreadful things that had happened to him and showed her the old lamp and fruits he had taken out of the underground garden.

His mother had no more idea of the great value of the beautiful fruits than he had, but, like him, thought they were made only of colored glass. When Aladdin had put them carelessly behind the cushions of the sofa, to be out of the way, she eagerly listened to the rest of his story, for she was full of indignation at the cruel conduct of the false uncle, but glad that her boy, whom she really loved, had escaped from so wicked a magician.

When Aladdin had come to the end of his story, he was only too glad to go to rest, since he was very tired after his adventures. On asking for some breakfast next morning he was grieved to learn that his poor mother had no food in the house. However, he told her not to be troubled, as he would take out the old lamp he had brought yesterday and sell it; they could buy at least a little food with the money he got for it.

His mother brought the lamp to him, and seeing that it was very dirty, she said she would clean it up a bit. But no sooner had she started rubbing the lamp than a most hideous genie of the largest size suddenly appeared before her, and said in a loud voice: "What wouldst thou have? I am ready to obey thee as thy slave, and the slave of all who have that lamp in their hands — I and the other slaves of the lamp!"

The poor woman was so dreadfully frightened at the sight of the genie that she fainted; but Aladdin snatched the lamp out of her hand and said: "I am hungry, bring me something to eat!"

The genie vanished, but instantly appeared again with a large silver tray, on which were twelve covered silver plates full of the richest foods. Then having also brought six large white loaves, two bottles of wine, and two silver cups, he placed the things on the floor and disappeared.

Aladdin now brought water, and sprinkling a little on her face, brought his mother out of her faint; then they both sat down to the splendid meal before them.

When Aladdin's mother presently learned that it was the dreadful genie who had brought these fine things she felt very uneasy and begged her son to be careful what he did, advising him to sell the lamp and the ring on his finger, and have nothing more to do with such magic things. But Aladdin told her that this would be a foolish thing to do, since they had already seen what wonders could be worked by means of these magic things. He said he would certainly keep the lamp, though he would hide it out of his mother's sight, since she was afraid of it, and the ring he meant to wear always on his finger, to help him when he was in danger.

So his mother said nothing more, and Aladdin put the lamp in a safe place, where he could easily find it again, and the ring he was careful to keep always on his finger.

When they had eaten all the food brought by the genie, Aladdin, determined not to suffer hunger any more, took one of the silver plates to a nearby dealer, and asked him if he would buy it. The man, seeing at once that the plate was really of great value, was ready enough to buy it, and offered a gold piece in exchange for it. Aladdin went away quite satisfied, having no idea that the plate was really worth very much more.

He bought food with the money, and when this was finished he took another silver plate to the dealer who paid him the same price again. By this means the poor window and her son, with care, were able to live in some comfort.

Now a great change for the better took place in Aladdin. His late strange adventures had the effect of changing him from a lazy careless lad into a steady sensible young man. He left off idling his time away with bad companions and began instead to speak with merchants and learned men, gleaning all he could from their talks and ways. By noticing how they conducted their business, he thus gained some knowledge of the world. Being by nature bright and clever, he soon began to improve very much, and in a short time no one could have recognized in him the idle good-for-nothing lad whom the cunning magician had chosen to serve his evil purposes.

When Aladdin had sold all the plates, even the great silver tray brought by the genie, and when the money he got for them was used up, he took the magic lamp once more and rubbed it. Instantly the genie appeared and asked what he desired. Upon Aladdin saying he was hungry, the hideous monster again brought him a silver tray full of dishes of food as before. When the food was finished Aladdin took the silver dishes, one by one, to be sold; but this time he met with one of the best goldsmiths in the city, who gave him sixty pieces of silver for each, which was their real value.

With this money Aladdin and his mother kept themselves comfortably for quite a long time, though they still lived in a very plain way. By talking with merchants and jewellers Aladdin soon learned another very surprising thing: He discovered that the beautiful fruits which he had taken out of the underground garden were not made of colored glass, as he had supposed, but were really precious jewels of untold value. But, though he was full of joy at this discovery, he kept it secret, even from his mother, at first.

It was just at this time that Aladdin first saw the sultan's daughter, the beautiful Princess Badroulbadour, and fell in love with her. Now it was quite against the law for any ordinary person to look upon the face of the princess; but Aladdin, hearing that she would pass by a certain part of the city one day, when everyone was expected to be out of the way, hid himself behind a door and managed to get a glimpse of her. He was so delighted with her great beauty that he loved her at once and felt he could never be happy unless he married her.

When he told his mother of this she only laughed at him and said he was foolish even to dream of such a thing, for the sultan would certainly never allow his daughter to be married to the son of a poor tailor. But Aladdin said he had quite made up his mind to marry the beautiful princess, and he begged his mother so hard to help him that at last she agreed to do so. So Aladdin brought out the pretty fruits he had gathered in the underground garden, told her that he had found out lately that they were really priceless jewels, and desired her to take them as a gift to the sultan, at the same time asking the hand of the Princess Badroulbadour in marriage. She said she would do so, and placing the jewels in a great china dish, she set out for the palace.

After some trouble she managed to get into the great hall where the sultan was dealing out justice to those who brought complaints before him; but everybody was too busy to take any notice of her. The next day she went again, but met with no better luck; and it was not until she had visited the palace for six days that the sultan, who had noticed the poor woman standing in the same place so patiently during this time, at last commanded that she should be brought up to the throne.

When Aladdin's mother came up to the throne she bowed low before the sultan, and humbly begged him to listen to what she had to say. She then told of the love that Aladdin had for the Princess Badroulbadour, and how greatly he desired to marry her, and at the same time she presented the sultan with the dish of jewel fruits that she had brought.

The sultan was so pleased with the dazzling beauty of these priceless gems that, far from being angry with the poor widow for daring to ask such a thing of him, he said that he would surely do well to give his daughter to a man who valued her at so high a price; but his grand vizier, who stood close at hand, advised him not to act too hastily. As it happened, the sultan had already half-promised his daughter to the grand vizier's son; so the minister now reminded him of this, asking him to wait three months longer before settling the matter, when his son would most likely be able to bring a more noble present even than that of Aladdin, who was an entire stranger.

The sultan agreed to this, and told Aladdin's mother to go home and tell her son that he accepted his offer, but could not let the princess be married until some special furniture was got ready for her, which would be finished in three months' time.

Aladdin was full of joy when he heard this good news, and was most eager for his wedding day to come. But he soon learnt that the sultan did not mean to keep his promise. One day his mother came rushing into the house, telling him that the streets were all decorated, and, upon asking the reason, she had just learned that it was because the Princess Badroulbadour was to be married that very night to the grand vizier's son.

This was a terrible disappointment for Aladdin, but still he was not without hope of getting the princess for himself after all. As soon as his mother had gone out of the room he took the magic lamp and rubbed it hard. As before, the genie appeared instantly and asked what he desired. Aladdin explained how unfairly he had been treated by the sultan, and then he desired the genie to help him by bringing the royal bride and bridegroom to his house that night. The genie promised to do so, and Aladdin felt satisfied.

The wedding rejoicings went on all evening, but no sooner had the princess and the vizier's son retired to rest in the palace, than the genie appeared, and raising the royal couch on to his shoulders, flew with it in an instant to Aladdin's house, where the princess was left in a dark room by herself, and the poor bridegroom was locked up in a cold dismal cellar all night.

When morning came they were taken back to the palace in the same astonishing manner, and as the whole adventure seemed like a dreadful dream, neither the princess nor the vizier's son said anything about it to the sultan.

When, however, the same thing happened again next night, they were both so much alarmed that they dared not keep the matter

E

a secret any longer. The vizier's son, seeing that magic was at work, said he would rather give up his bride than go through such a night again and be the means of bringing trouble upon the princess.

On hearing what had taken place, the sultan, agreeing with the vizier's son, at once ordered all the wedding rejoicings to be stopped, and the marriage declared not to have taken place. Aladdin was full of joy to find how well his plan had worked, knowing that the beautiful princess was once more free to become his own bride.

However, he waited till the three months the sultan had asked were over; then he sent his mother once more to the palace to ask again for the princess' hand in marriage.

The sultan at once recognized the widow, and listened quietly to what she had to say; but as the grand vizier again advised him to take time, he told her that Aladdin should marry his daughter only on condition that he sent him first as a present forty golden basins full of the same sort of priceless jewels he had sent before, carried by forty black slaves led by the same number of white slaves, all of whom were to be richly dressed!

The widow went sadly home, feeling sure that her son would now have to give up all idea of marrying the princess, since he would never be able to send such a present to the sultan. But Aladdin did not lose hope: As soon as his mother left him he rubbed his wonderful lamp, and the genie again stood before him.

He quickly explained what he wanted as a gift for the sultan, and in a very short time the genie returned with forty splendidly dressed tall handsome slaves, followed by forty more slaves, bearing on their heads solid golden basins full of diamonds, pearls, rubies, emeralds, and other precious stones, all of which were even larger and more beautiful than those taken from the underground garden.

The slaves quite filled Aladdin's little house and garden. When it had learned that nothing more was wanted, the genie vanished.

Aladdin was quite delighted, and sent the slaves at once to the palace, persuading his mother to follow in their train, to present them to the sultan in his name.

When the slaves arrived at the palace they made a great stir, for none of the lords or ladies had ever before beheld such splendid servants; and when the sultan saw the golden basins full of dazzling jewels, which they laid at his feet, he was delighted and felt that he could not do better than give his daughter to so rich a suitor.

So he told Aladdin's mother that her son should now certainly marry the princess, and that the sooner he came to fetch her the better he would be pleased.

Quickly the widow hurried back home with this good news, and Aladdin once more took his magic lamp and brought the genie before him. This time he asked the genie to dress him in rich clothes, fit for the most splendid king, and to bring him the finest horse in the world to ride upon, with twenty slaves to go before him, and twenty slaves to follow him, all as richly clothed as those he had sent to the sultan. Besides this, he ordered that six gaily dressed female slaves, each carrying gorgeous robes fit for a queen, should be brought for his mother; and he also asked the genie to leave him ten thousand pieces of gold in ten purses.

When all these things had been brought, and the genie had vanished, Aladdin, dressed magnificently and looking like a handsome young prince on his prancing horse, set off for the palace, with his mother and the slaves following in a grand procession. As he thus rode along in state, he gave orders to certain of the slaves to throw showers of gold pieces among the crowds of people who stood in the streets to watch him go by.

In this manner, followed by the cheers of the crowd, Aladdin arrived at the palace, where he was received as a prince by the sultan, who was now ready for the marriage to take place that very day.

But Aladdin said he could not think of taking the Princess Badroulbadour away from her father until he had built a splendid palace for her to live in; and he asked the sultan to allow him a space to set up such a building, within sight of his own palace.

To this the sultan gladly agreed. After a most splendid feast, Aladdin returned to his home, where he quickly called the genie of the lamp to his aid once more.

He now asked the genie to build, opposite to

that of the sultan, a magnificent palace, the walls of which were to be made of solid gold and silver, and the windows, doors, and pillars of which were to be decorated and covered with pearls, diamonds, rubies, and every kind of precious stone. The inside was to be furnished in the most gorgeous style. Slaves, lords, and ladies, all splendidly dressed, were to be ready to wait in every room. A great treasure of gold and silver was to be laid in a certain secret part, known to Aladdin only, who also told the genie to be sure to leave one of the large jeweled windows unfinished.

Having thus given his orders, Aladdin went to bed. When he awoke next morning he found that the genie had indeed caused a wonderful palace, even more gorgeous than anything he could ever have imagined, to be built for him in the place he had named. He and his mother at once took up their abode there.

When the sultan beheld from his own windows this dazzling palace, sparkling and glittering in the sunlight with priceless jewels and fine gold, he was amazed and delighted beyond measure. On that very evening the marriage of his daughter with Aladdin took place in splendid state, and the greatest rejoicings were held in the city.

Next day the sultan himself entered the jewel palace, to admire it more closely, and then it was that he noticed that one of the windows had been left unfinished. When he asked the reason for this, Aladdin said that this had been done by his orders, as he wished to give the sultan the pleasure of putting the finishing touch to the wonderful palace himself.

The sultan was pleased with the idea, and at once sent for his chief jewelers, bidding them finish the window with gems in the same manner as the others in the palace.

The jewelers set to work without delay, but though they did their best, at the end of a month the window was not half-finished, and they were at a standstill for want of jewels, having used up all that the sultan and even his grand vizier had.

Then Aladdin, who had known all along that their work would be in vain, and who had only wished to prove still further that he was even richer and more powerful than the sultan himself, ordered the jewelers to undo their work, and take their jewels away again. He then called the genie into his presence, and desired him to finish the window in the same manner as the others. This was done instantly; and when the sultan saw this fresh proof of Aladdin's power, he was more pleased with him than ever.

Now that Aladdin had gained the very height of his wishes, being married to the beautiful Princess Badroulbadour, and living the life of a splendid prince, he was perfectly happy. But after a while trouble once more came upon him.

The wicked magician was still alive. Having learned by means of his magic that Aladdin had not died in the cave, but was living happily the life of a prince, and still had the wonderful lamp in his keeping, he became very angry and jealous. After a while he made up his mind to go back to China and try once more to get the magic lamp for himself, and, if possible, to destroy Aladdin's happiness. So he set off and soon arrived in the city where Aladdin lived. In a very short time he found out all he could about his doings and the wonderful power that he had in the land.

Having learned that Aladdin himself was at present away hunting in the country, he thought of a cunning plan for stealing the magic lamp before he came back. Dressing himself up as a poor merchant, he bought a basket full of small lamps, and then went from street to street, calling out:

"New lamps for old lamps! Who will change old lamps for new ones?"

Even the children in the streets laughed at him for making such a foolish offer; but the magician heeded them not, and soon came crying his wares before the dazzling windows of Aladdin's splendid palace.

It happened that one of the princess' ladies noticed him, and going at once to her mistress she said: "There is a foolish fellow outside who says he will give new lamps in exchange for old ones! I have seen in Prince Aladdin's room a dirty old lamp that can surely be of no use. Shall I take it down to the merchant and ask him to give me a new one for it?"

The Princess Badroulbadour, having no idea of the real value of the magic lamp, laughed and said she might do so if she chose; so the lady-in-waiting took the old lamp down to the pretended merchant, who eagerly grabbed it, and gave her a fine new one in exchange for it.

No sooner had the magician left the palace and made his way to a lonely spot, then seeing that the lamp was indeed the one he sought, he rubbed it hard and the genie instantly appeared, ready to obey him as the owner of the lamp. To him the magician said: "Carry me, together with Aladdin's palace, with the princess and all within it, into the middle of Africa!" These words were hardly spoken when the genie obeyed them to the letter, and in an instant the magician and Aladdin's palace were set down in a lonely plain in the heart of Africa.

Next morning, when the sultan arose, he was astonished and terribly upset to find that the dazzling jewel palace, with his beloved daughter and all within it, had entirely vanished. Full of rage and grief he sent soldiers to meet Aladdin on his return from hunting and had him brought as a captive before him.

Aladdin was even more shocked and grieved at what had happened than the sultan, who was eager to have him beheaded at once. His great love for the princess made Aladdin hope that he might yet save her from danger, and he begged the sultan to allow him forty days in which to search for her. If at the end of that time he should meet with no success, he would gladly give up his life.

The sultan agreed to this, and Aladdin began his search; but he seemed so dazed and helpless that he could scarcely think, and many people began to look upon him as mad.

After rushing wildly about the city for several days, searching in vain for the princess and for news of his palace, poor Aladdin wandered out into the country, where he flung himself down on the bank of the river, in the utmost grief, feeling that his task was quite hopeless, and that he might as well drown himself.

He was just about to say his prayers for the last time when he suddenly slipped down the bank, and in grasping hold of a rock to save himself he happened to rub the magic ring which the magician had given him, and which he had worn on his finger so constantly that he had forgotten about its powers for the time being. However, he found it of great service now; for no sooner had he rubbed it against the rock than there appeared the same genie as he had seen in the cave, who at once asked for his commands.

Very pleasantly surprised, Aladdin asked for his palace to be brought back to its place in the city. But the genie said he could not quite do this, since that power belonged only to the genie of the lamp; so Aladdin asked instead to be set down beneath the window of the princess' room in the palace wherever it might be.

In an instant Aladdin found himself in the midst of a lonely plain in Africa, standing outside his own splendid palace.

It was night when he arrived; but early in the morning the Princess Badroulbadour looked out of her window. Seeing Aladdin outside in the garden, she was full of delight and sent for him to be brought to her at once.

Aladdin was overjoyed to find himself with his beautiful princess once more, and he quickly asked her to tell him all she knew of the dreadful thing that had happened to them both, and also if she knew what had become of the old lamp which he kept in his own room. The princess explained how she had allowed the old lamp to be exchanged for a new one, and was greatly surprised now to learn of its real value. She also stated how frightened she had been on waking up to find herself so suddenly in Africa and far away from anyone's help.

Aladdin next asked for news of the magician, who he now knew had played him this trick. The princess said that the wicked sorcerer came to see her once every day, being eager to marry her himself, but that she always treated him with such scorn that he did not care to come oftener.

On learning that the magician carried the lamp about with him, hidden in his clothes, Aladdin now thought out a careful plan: He told the princess to overcome her dislike so far as to invite the sorcerer to have supper with her that night and to give him a cup of wine, in whch a certain poison should be mixed.

The princess gladly agreed to do this and sent an invitation at once to the magician to come to supper with her that night, while Aladdin quickly made his way to the nearest city, where he bought a deadly drug, and returned with it to the palace. He mixed the poison in a cup of wine, which he told the princess to entice the magician to drink during supper time; then he hid himself in another room to await the end of his plan.

The magician came in good time to the supper, and was quite delighted to find the princess beautifully dressed and waiting with smiles to receive him. They sat down to quite a splendid feast, and talked and laughed together in the most friendly manner. When the princess at last offered the magician the cup of poisoned wine, he drank it off without any fear, as he had done the other wine before. But no sooner had the wicked sorcerer taken that deadly drink then he fell over on the couch quite lifeless.

Aladdin now rushed into the room. Searching among the dead magician's clothes, to his joy he found the magic lamp, and then quickly rubbing it, he brought the genie before him and desired that the palace should be set down in its proper place in China once again.

This was instantly done — you can imagine the surprise and the joy of the sultan when he again set eyes on Aladdin's palace and knew that his dear daughter was still alive and safe within.

The greatest rejoicings were kept up all over the country for a very long time, in honor of the return of the princess. But even now Aladdin was not out of danger.

It happened that the African magician had a younger brother, who had also studied magic, and who, having learned by his arts what had happened to his brother, at once set off for China to take revenge on Aladdin.

Having arrived in the city, he soon thought out a clever plan: Hearing of a certain holy woman, named Fatima, whose goodness had caused her to be much respected and beloved by the people, he went to the cell where she lived all alone. Here he very soon killed poor Fatima, and dressing himself up in her clothes, he passed himself off as the holy woman.

In this manner he made his way through the city to Aladdin's palace, and got himself brought before the Princess Badroulbadour.

The princess, having heard much about the holy woman, begged the pretended Fatima to remain in the palace, that she might learn from her how to be truly good. This was settled; and later the princess took her new friend into the splendid hall of the palace and asked her what she thought of it.

The false Fatima said it was truly noble and needed but one thing to make it the most splendid hall in the world. When asked by the princess to name this thing, she said that if a roc's egg were hung up in the golden dome it would indeed be quite perfect.

The wicked magician said this because he knew that if Aladdin asked for a roc's egg, the genie would be very angry and would most likely kill him, for the roc was a magic bird, and was served by genii. But the princess did not know this, and when next she saw Aladdin she asked him to order that a roc's egg should be hung up in the hall.

So Aladdin rubbed the magic lamp, and commanded the genie to hang a roc's egg up in the golden dome. On hearing this the genie flew into a great rage, saying that Aladdin deserved to be destroyed for asking such a thing, after all that had already been done for him.

Aladdin was much alarmed, for he did not even know what a roc was; but the genie, seeing that he had not really meant to offend him, explained that the so-called holy woman was really the magician's brother and advised Aladdin to be on his guard.

So when the genie had vanished, Aladdin went to the princess' room, where, pretending to have a bad headache, he caused the holy woman to be sent for, to see if she could cure it.

No sooner, however, did the false Fatima draw near him than Aladdin seized his dagger and stabbed her, so that she fell down dead.

The princess was at first shocked that her husband had killed the holy woman; but Aladdin soon explained his reason to her, and showed how the woman was really the African magician's wicked brother, who had meant to kill them both.

After this there was no danger to be feared. Aladdin and his beautiful princess settled down to live in happiness and splendor; and when at length the sultan of China died, Aladdin and his beautiful wife reigned together in peace for the rest of their lives.

## Ali Baba
## and the Forty Thieves

ONCE UPON A TIME THERE LIVED IN A
certain town of Persia two brothers, whose
names were Ali Baba and Cassim. These two,
although they were brothers, were not alike in
any way, nor were they on the best of terms.
Now Cassim was rich, and Ali Baba was very
poor. What little means their father had
was divided equally between them at his
death; but Cassim, by marrying a rich wife,
became a great merchant and was able to live
in much comfort. Ali Baba's wife, though
she loved him well, brought him no riches at
all and was as badly off as himself. So he
still remained a poor man, gaining a wretched
living by cutting wood in a forest near by
and carrying it about the town to sell on three
asses, which made up the whole of his wealth.

Although Ali Baba was so poor, he was of a
much better and kinder disposition than his
more fortunate brother; for Cassim was
haughty, unloving, and grasping, and at last
his great greediness brought sad trouble upon
him, as you will see.

One day, Ali Baba went out into the forest as usual, to cut wood, taking with him his three asses to carry home the results of his hard work. He had just finished his humble task, having cut as much wood as his asses could carry, when suddenly he noticed in the distance a great cloud of dust, which seemed to be moving toward him. He looked at it very carefully and soon saw that it was caused by a body of men galloping swiftly along on horseback.

Now Ali Baba was by no means a dull man, for he had his wits about him; thinking that these strange horsemen might perhaps prove to be fierce robbers, he quickly made up his mind to keep out of their way. Seeing a large tree growing beside a steep craggy rock close at hand, he climbed up into the midst of it, so that though he was completely hidden from sight, yet he could see what the horsemen were doing down below.

The party came forward at a great rate, and to the surprise and dismay of Ali Baba they drew rein close to his hiding place. The poor woodcutter took a good look at the men as they dismounted and tied their horses to the trees and shrubs around. Judging from their wild fierce looks and the heavy bags which they carried, he felt quite sure that they must be robbers. Nor indeed was he wrong in his guess, for they were none other than a band of robbers who carried on their plundering some distance away and had their meeting place at that spot.

He counted forty of them altogether, and

noticed that one, who had the finest appearance, seemed to be their captain or leader, since he gave orders, which the others obeyed. When they had all tied up their horses, this man came forward, and standing in front of the great rock beside which Ali Baba's tree stood, he called out these words: *"Open, Sesame!"*

Ali Baba bent forward with breathless eagerness, and to his great astonishment, as soon as the robber captain spoke these words, a door flew open in the rock. The forty men, carrying their heavy bags on their shoulders, all marched through the opening, and then the door shut of its own accord.

Ali Baba did not dare to stir from his hiding place for fear the robbers should suddenly come out and see him, so he waited patiently where he was for some time, until at last the door in the rock flew open once more.

The robbers all trooped out, with empty bags this time, and quickly mounted their horses. Their captain, after saying *"Shut, Sesame!"* upon which the door closed, placed himself at the head of them, and they all rode off.

Having waited until the robbers were quite a long way off, Ali Baba came down from his tree; and then being very curious to know what was to be seen on the other side of the door in the rock, he made up his mind to try to enter. He remembered the words that the robber captain had used; so making his way through the bushes, he stood before the rock, and cried: *"Open, Sesame!"* The door flew open at once; and as soon as the woodcutter entered, it shut of its own accord.

Ali Baba was surprised to find himself in a large cave, well-lighted from an opening at the top, and full of wonderful treasures on every side. There were bales of silk and rich clothes, handsome carpets piled one above another, great heaps of solid gold and silver in heavy bars; to say nothing of fat bulging bags full of money and priceless jewels, which filled every odd space.

The poor woodcutter at once guessed that this cave had been the home and storehouse of robbers for a great many years; and since the treasures had already been stolen in the first place, probably years ago, he did not think it wrong to help himself now. So he quickly gathered together as many of the bags of gold as he thought his three asses could carry and got them safely outside, being careful to say the words *"Shut, Sesame!"* when he came out for the last time, so that the robbers would find the door in the rock closed when they came again, and would not know that their hiding place was discovered.

Then he found his asses, which had strayed to some little distance, and loaded them with the bags of gold, over which he carefully piled wood, so that they were hidden. When all was ready he went back to town.

When he got to the wretched hut that was his home, he took the bags inside and poured out the gold in a great shining heap upon the floor.

His poor wife was full of surprise and delight at this beautiful sight. She listened in amazement to the wonderful tale that Ali Baba had to tell, and when he had finished, she was eager to count the money. But Ali Baba said this would take too long a time, for he wanted to bury the money in the garden at once, thinking it better to keep his new riches a secret at present, since he did not wish others to know of the treasure house he had found.

However, his wife said that she would at least weigh the gold, while he was digging the hole for it; and since she had not a measure of her own large enough, she went to the house of Cassim, her brother-in-law, to borrow one.

Now Cassim's wife was curious to know what Ali Baba and his wife could want to measure in such a hurry, seeing that they were so very poor, so she took the trouble to smear the bottom of the measure with fat, which would tell her what kind of corn had been weighed in it, since some of the grains would most likely get buried in the fat.

Ali Baba's wife quickly took the measure to her own house, and not noticing the fat at the bottom, carefully weighed the gold. She then took the measure back, and her husband buried his treasure.

As soon as Cassim's wife was alone she looked at the measure and noticed a small piece of gold that had stuck to the fat at the bottom. She was filled with envy at the thought that Ali Baba, who she had always understood to be so poor, had so much gold as to need to measure it.

When her husband came home she showed him the piece of money she had found in the measure. Cassim, instead of being pleased that his brother, at one time very poor, was now evidently rich, became so full of rage and jealousy that he could not sleep all night.

Directly morning came he went to Ali Baba to demand how it came about that he had so much money as to need to weigh it; and he showed him the piece of gold found in the measure.

Ali Baba saw that he could not keep his secret from his brother, so he told Cassim all about the robbers' cave, and of his adventure on the day before.

Now Cassim was a very greedy man indeed, and although he was already quite rich enough, he wanted to be still richer; so, as he had never behaved kindly to his brother, he now very haughtily ordered Ali Baba to tell him exactly where the robbers' cave was to be found, or he would tell the rulers of the town that his brother was a thief, and so get him into trouble.

Ali Baba was thus obliged to tell his unkind brother all he wished, even to the very words that would open the door in the rock; then greedy Cassim went away, making up his mind to visit the cave at once and take away all the treasures for himself, so that his brother could get no more.

So early next morning, before anyone else was awake, he set off with ten mules loaded with empty chests to hold the treasure and quickly made his way along the paths that Ali Baba had told him to take. In this manner he soon found the rock, and standing before it, he uttered the magic words: *"Open, Sesame!"*

The door flew open as he had been told it would, and when he stepped inside the cave it closed again. Cassim was full of astonishment and delight, for even his greedy mind had never dreamed of such wonderful riches as he saw on every side of him.

He soon set to work to drag as many of the bags of gold as he could lift toward the door; but his thoughts were so full of his new riches, and of the fine figure he would cut with them, that when he was ready to go he could not think of the magic word that would open the door for him.

Now sesame is a certain kind of grain, and Cassim knew that the word he had forgotten was the name of corn of some kind; but try as he would, he could not remember the exact word. He said: *"Open, Barley,"* and cried out the name of every other kind of grain he could remember; but none of these was the right word, and so the door remained shut.

The more he tried to remember the word, the more confused he got; at last he threw down the moneybags he held in his hands, and rushed about the cave in despair, trying to find another way out. But all his efforts were in vain. When, at noon, he heard the noise of galloping horses, which told him the robbers were returning, he was full of fear and felt that his last hour had come.

However, Cassim made up his mind to try and escape, so when at length the door flew open at the magic word "*Sesame*," which he had not been able to remember, he rushed out and tried to get away. But the robbers saw him at once, and seizing the wretched man, they soon killed him with their sabers.

The robbers were much alarmed to find that their hiding place had been discovered, and they could not imagine how Cassim could have got into the cave, since they had always thought that no one but themselves knew of the magic phrase which would open the door. Fearing lest the man whom they had just killed might have shared the secret with others, they cut his dead body into four pieces, hanging two quarters on either side of the cave door, to frighten anyone else who might be so bold as to enter. When they had done this, they once more mounted their horses and rode away to rob all whom they met.

When Cassim's wife found that her husband did not return home at nightfall, she was afraid that something dreadful must have happened to him; early next morning she went to Ali Baba to tell him of her fears. Ali Baba did what he could to comfort her; and then forgetting all about his brother's greediness and unkind behavior to himself, he at once set off, with his three asses, to find out what had become of him.

When he came to the robbers' hiding place, he stood beside the rock and called out:

*"Open, Sesame!"* and the door flew open as before. The first sight that met his eyes was Cassim's divided body. Full of horror at his brother's sad end, he took down the four pieces, and wrapping them up, he placed them on one of his asses to take home with him. Then he loaded the other two asses with bags of gold, covering them over with wood as before; and when he had again named the magic word that closed the door of the cave, he started off home once more, being careful to wait at the end of the forest until night had set in, that he might pass through the town in the dark.

Having put his new treasures in safety, he went on to his sister-in-law's house, taking Cassim's dead body with him. The door was opened by a clever and beautiful young slave girl, named Morgiana, whom Ali Baba well knew could be trusted with a secret; so he told her of what happened to her master, saying that the manner of his death must be kept a secret and that this friends must be told that he had died in a natural way. Morgiana promised to do all she could to carry out this plan; and then she went to call her mistress.

When Cassim's wife saw her husband's dead body, and heard how he had met with his death, she was in great grief; but Ali Baba soon thought of a way to comfort her. He said that he himself was ready to marry her and share his new riches with her, if she would keep the secret of the robbers' cave, and let her friends think that Cassim had died a natural death. Since it was a custom of the country for a man to marry his brother's widow and take her to live with his own wife, there was nothing strange in the offer.

So Cassim's widow, feeling lonely and knowing that her brother-in-law was now a very rich man, was quite willing to become his wife. Being greatly comforted by the thought that she would still be cared for, she agreed to all the plans of Ali Baba, and promised to keep the true manner of Cassim's death a secret.

Now Morgiana was really a very clever girl indeed, and she soon thought of a fine plan to help her mistress in this matter. As soon as Ali Baba had returned to his own home, she went out to a shop where medicines were sold, and asked for some special lozenges very good in case of bad illness. When the man in the shop asked who was ill at Cassim's house she told him that it was her master himself, and that he was in a very bad state indeed. Next morning she went again to the same shop, and bought a certain medicine only given to sick persons likely to die, saying she feared her master would not get better now. As Ali Baba and his wife also went many times back and forth with sad faces between the two houses, no one was surprised, when evening came, to learn that Cassim was dead; and all were ready to believe that he had died in the ordinary way.

The next thing to be done was to dispose of the dead body so that no one should find out that it had been cut into four pieces; but

Morgiana was not at a loss. Early next morning she went to the stall of an old cobbler, named Baba Mustapha, who she knew would be at work before anyone else was up. Putting a piece of gold into his hand, she asked him to take his needle and thread and go with her to do some important work, saying however that she must blindfold him at the end of the street, for she did not wish him to know where she was taking him.

Baba Mustapha at first did not like the idea of such a strange errand; but he was a merry obliging old fellow, and when Morgiana put another piece of gold in his hand and promised him a third piece when his task was done, he agreed to go with her. They set off at once, and at the end of the street Morgiana tied a handkerchief over the old cobbler's eyes and did not take it off until she had brought him into the very room where her dead master's quartered body lay.

Then she told him to take his needle and thread and carefully sew the pieces together. When he had finished, she gave him a third piece of gold and blindfolding him again, she led him back to his own street, going in a very roundabout way, up and down many streets, in order to confuse him, and feeling satisfied that he could not know where he had been.

Now that Cassim's body had been put together again, it was buried in the usual way, without anyone discovering the secret of his death. A few days later, Ali Baba took his wife and belongings and went to live in his brother's house. A short time after, he married

Cassim's widow, as he had promised, and began to enjoy his new-found riches.

In the meantime, the forty thieves were beginning to feel very uneasy. When they came back to their cave and saw that Cassim's dead body had been taken away, together with some of their treasure bags, they knew for certain that someone else knew of their hiding place. The captain, fearing that they were in danger of being captured, suggested that one of the band should go disguised into the town at the end of the forest and try to find out all he could from the people's talk about the man they had killed, since it was evident his friends would know of the manner in which he had met his death.

One of the robbers willingly offered to do as the captain asked, even when he was told that if he gave their secret to anyone, or failed in his task, he would be killed. After dressing himself in such a way that no one could guess that he was a fierce robber, he said good-bye to his companions and set out, entering the town just at daybreak.

No one was about so early in the day, but, as it happened, the spy walked past the stall of the cobbler, Baba Mustapha, who was always up betimes. Seeing the old fellow already at work, he bid him good day, saying that he must have good eyesight if he could see to work when the daylight was still so faint.

The cobbler replied that his eyes were indeed very good, for it was not long ago that he had managed to sew up a dead body in a room where there was even less light than he had at present.

When the robber heard this, he was full of joy, for he felt sure he had got on the right track straightaway; but he pretended to be much surprised, and putting a piece of gold into the old cobbler's hand, he asked him to point out the house where he had done such a strange piece of work.

Baba Mustapha said he could not do this, since he had been led blindfold to the house, and did not know what streets he had passed through; but when the robber put another piece of gold into his hand, and suggested that perhaps Baba Mustapha could find the house again if he were led blindfold once more, the tailor, eager for gold, agreed to try. Thrusting the coin into his pocket, he tied a kerchief over his eyes and then said, "I am ready, sir." The tailor put his hand on the robber's arm, and in this way the pair passed through the streets.

Baba Mustapha was a very clever man, and he could tell just where he was going by the touch of his feet on the roughness or smoothness of the ground. He could tell by the sounds that he heard and even by the odors he smelled. So it was that when they passed by a shop where a parrot squawked and talked, Baba Mustapha, remembering that he had heard just such a bird when he had been led blindfolded before, knew now that he was proceeding in the right direction.

After they had been walking along for some time, the tailor paused and tugged at the sleeve of the robber. "Stop here, sir," he said. "I think it was this far I traveled when I came with the young woman." And they were in front of Cassim's house, where Ali Baba now lived. The robber-spy took a piece of chalk and with it carefully marked the door of the house, for in this way he would be able once more to find the place by himself.

Then he removed the kerchief from Baba Mustapha's eyes and said, "Many thanks for this favor, little tailor. May Allah preserve and guide you. But before you go, can you tell me who it is that lives in this house?"

The tailor only shook his head and replied that he did not know that part of the city well. Thanking him again, the robber-spy dismissed him and then hurried off to report what he had discovered.

Soon after, Morgiana, going out of the house on an errand, noticed and wondered at the chalk marks on the door. Could it be that some enemy of the master's had left these signs?

Fearing that someone wished to harm her master, Morgiana tried to think of a way in which she could protect him from any evil his enemies might be planning. At last she said to herself, "I know how I shall fool whoever has done this." So saying, she took a piece of chalk and put on the door of every neighboring house the same kind of mark as the robber-spy had made. The slave girl said nothing of this to anyone.

Meanwhile the robber told the captain of the thieves how in the city there was a tailor who claimed to have sewn up a body and how the tailor had led him to the house where the body had been. "I have marked the door of that house, my captain. Thus we can know it."

"Let us all go into the city then," replied the leader of the thieves. "Later on, after this man and I have found the house we are seeking, we shall meet at the square. I shall then tell you what next is to be done." And the robbers set off without delay.

The captain and the spy, upon entering the city, soon found the street in which Ali Baba lived, but they could not tell which was the right house, since they found a number of doors marked with chalk in the same way. The spy was full of dismay when he saw what a trick had been played upon him. Fearing the captain's anger, he declared that he had marked only one of the doors, and had quite expected to know the house again by means of that mark. But the captain only led the way to the great square where the other robbers were already waiting. Telling them that their plan had completely failed, he said they must return to the forest, for they could do nothing more that day.

When the robbers were once more safe in their cave, they killed the spy who had failed in his work; and then as their danger was as great as ever, another of the troop offered to seek out their enemy's house, although the captain promised that he also should die if he failed as the other had done. This second offer was gladly accepted and the new spy set out.

He went straight to Baba Mustapha's stall, and, by giving him plenty of gold, persuaded the old cobbler to be blindfolded once more, and to lead the way to Ali Baba's house. When they arrived there the robber took a piece of red chalk he had brought with him, and marked the door in an out-of-the-way place, feeling sure he would thus know it again. Then he let the cobbler go back to his stall, and returned to the forest cave.

When the second spy declared that he could certainly point out the house where their enemy lived, the robbers were pleased, and decided to enter the town again in the same manner as before. But when the captain and the spy came into the street they were once more disappointed, for Morgiana's keen eyes had noticed the red chalk mark on her master's door, and by carefully marking the neighboring doors in exactly the same way and place with red chalk also, she had again spoiled the robber's plan.

The captain and his men returned to the forest in an awful rage, and when they got to their cave they quickly killed the second spy for having failed in his task.

Now the robber captain, not wishing to lose any more of his fine troop in this way, said that he himself would go alone into the town and see if he could succeed better; so he disguised himself and set off.

As the other spies had done, he went to the old cobbler, Baba Mustapha, who, for the sake of more gold, was willing to be blindfolded once again and to lead the robber to Ali Baba's house. When he got there the captain did not mark the door at all, but looked well at the house, noting exactly at what part of the street it lay, and walking past it many times, so that he knew he could not fail to find it when next he came.

Then he went back to the cave and told his men that he had thought of a fine plan for doing away with their enemy, and he bade them go in small parties into the villages round about, and buy nineteen mules and thirty-eight very large leather jars, one of them was to be full of oil, and the rest to be empty.

In a few days the mules and jars were all bought, and then the captain set to work to carry out the plan he had thought of. He put a robber into each of the empty leather jars, rubbing the outside with oil, and covering over the tops, but leaving a little opening for air to get in. Then he loaded each mule with two of the jars, one on either side, taking care to carry the jar of real oil with him as well, in case anyone might wish to look at his goods.

When all was ready, he dressed himself up as a merchant and set out with his loaded mules, arriving in the town just as it was growing dusk. He led them on purpose through the street where his enemy lived, and when he came up to the right house he was pleased to find Ali Baba himself sitting outside the door, enjoying the cool evening air.

He at once left his mules and went to speak

to Ali Baba, saying that he was a merchant and had brought oil from a great distance to sell in the market next day, but that it was now so late he did not care to go farther into the town; and he asked Ali Baba if he might pass the night with him.

Ali Baba did not recognize the disguised robber-captain, but thinking that the stranger before him was a respectable oil merchant, he said he was welcome to spend the night with him. He at once sent a slave to lead the mules into the yard at the back of the house and to unload them there, while he himself went to Morgiana to bid her get ready a good supper for his guest. At first the sham merchant did not wish to enter Ali Baba's house, thinking he might carry out his plan better if he passed the night in the yard; but Ali Baba would not hear of this, and so he was obliged to do as his host wished.

A fine supper was quickly served, and while his guest feasted, Ali Baba talked pleasantly to him. But at last he went away to say something to Morgiana, and at the same time the robber-captain stepped into the yard to look at his mules, so he said, but really to speak to his men. He warned them that when they heard him throw some stones into the yard from his chamber window at a certain time during the night, they were to cut open with their knives the leather bags in which they were hidden, to step out and wait until he joined them. When he had whispered these directions into each jar, he returned to the house, and Morgiana took him to the room where he was to sleep. This room, as it happened, overlooked the yard.

Now Ali Baba had told Morgiana that as he intended to go to the baths very early next morning, she was to put out his bathing garments ready for him, and to make him some nice broth to take when he returned. Before going to rest, the careful slave did what her master bade her. She put out the bathing garments, and began to make the broth; but while she was doing this the lamp went out, and since there was no more oil in the house she did not know how she would finish her work.

The man-slave, Abdalla, seeing what a fix she was in, told her to go into the yard and take a little oil from one of the great jars the merchant had brought. So Morgiana, thinking this to be good advice, took her oil-pot and went out into the yard. But great was her surprise on reaching the first jar to hear a voice from within say these words in a very soft tone: "Is it time?"

Now most maidens would have screamed and made a great fuss on finding a man in a jar which was supposed to be full of oil. But Morgiana was wise and not easily frightened. Understanding at once that she had surprised some secret that meant danger to her master's household, she kept quiet and answered in an equally low tone: "Not yet, but presently!" She then went to each of the jars in turn, and whispered the same answer, until she came to the last, which she found to be full of oil.

Having discovered that a band of robbers

were in the yard, only waiting for word from their leader, the supposed merchant, to do some dreadful deed, Morgiana felt that her beloved master and his household were in great danger, and that it rested with her alone to save them since everyone else was in bed. She therefore made up her mind to lose no time, and thought out a clever plan.

Very quickly she made up a big fire in the kitchen. Taking her largest kettle, she filled it with oil from the jar outside and put it on to boil. As soon as it was ready, she took the kettle into the yard and quickly poured just enough of the boiling oil into each of the jars to kill the man inside. She did this so suddenly and so quietly that the robbers had not time to call out before they were smothered, and so no noise was made. After preparing her master's broth, Morgiana put out the lights, and waited to see what would happen next.

In a short time she saw the pretended merchant, whom she now knew to be the captain of the thieves, come to his chamber window and throw some pebbles onto the jars in the yard. He did this several times. Finding that his men did not stir, he grew alarmed, and crept softly down into the yard to see what was the matter. He looked into each of the jars and saw that all his men were dead. He smelled the boiling oil that had been poured over them, and knew that his fine plan for destroying and robbing Ali Baba and his household had been found out and spoiled. Full of rage, he made his way into the garden and escaped over the walls.

When Morgiana saw that the robber-captain was now safely out of the way, she herself went to rest, without saying a word to anyone of what had happened.

Next morning when Ali Baba returned from the baths, he was surprised to find the jars of oil still in the yard, for he had expected that the merchant would have gone at daybreak, so as to be early at the market. So he asked Morgiana what this meant.

Morgiana took her master into the yard, and showing him the dead men in the jars, told him the whole story of the wicked plot she had discovered and spoiled. She also told him for the first time about the chalk marks she had seen before on the door, and which she now knew to be connected with this plot of the forest robbers.

When Ali Baba heard this strange story, he was full of surprise. He felt so grateful to Morgiana, who by her cleverness and bravery had saved his life and the lives of all his household, that he decided that as a reward for what she had done, she should be a slave no longer. He then called Abdalla, and the two of them set to work to bury the dead robbers secretly in the garden, that no one might know of the strange thing that had happened. By selling the mules at different times, and living in a quiet manner, he prevented people from talking about him, and from guessing how he became rich in so short a time.

In the meantime, the robber-captain went back to his cave, angry because his plan had failed, and full of grief at the loss of his companions. He wondered how he would ever manage to get such a fine troop of men together again; but before seeking out a new band to guard his treasures, he made up his mind to try once more to destroy Ali Baba, who he felt would be a danger to him as long as he lived, since he knew the secret of the cave.

So next day he disguised himself again. Carrying a number of rich silks and stuffs with him, he went into the town; and taking a lodging and warehouse, he began business as a cloth merchant, under the false name of Cogia Houssain. The warehouse he had taken was next door to that in which Ali Baba's son did business, and he had chosen it for this very reason; for he hoped to become friendly with the young man and to use him in carrying out his evil plan.

By behaving well and being pleasant, the supposed merchant, Cogia Houssain, soon became very friendly with all the people round about, especially with Ali Baba's son, whom he treated most kindly, often inviting him to dine at his house and loading him with favors; so much so, indeed, that the young man was eager to make some return to his new friend. He spoke to his father about this, saying he would like to invite Cogia Houssain to dine with him, but that his own house was not large or fine enough to entertain such a guest in the way he wished. Then Ali Baba said that he himself would be glad to receive his son's friend, and advised him to walk out with Gogia Houssain some time and call in on their way back, as this would look more friendly than sending him a formal invitation.

On the following day, the young man asked Cogia Houssain to walk out with him; and when they came to Ali Baba's house, he asked the merchant to enter, saying his father was most eager to know him. The robber, though he meant to enter this house and kill his enemy some time or other, had not yet made his plans, and so did not wish to accept the invitation; but Ali Baba's son would not hear of him going away, and, taking him by the hand, insisted on bringing him into his father's house.

Ali Baba received his son's friend with great favor, and said that he must remain to supper; but the false merchant asked to be excused, saying he had a good reason for not staying to supper. When he was asked to state his reason, he said that he could not eat any food with salt in it; but Ali Baba said that this did not matter, for he would give orders that no salt should be put into the food that would be served for supper.

Now it is a custom in the East, where the scene of this story is laid, for one who has eaten of another's salt to be obliged to be friendly to that person and to do well by him; and so the robber-captain thought that if he ate salt in Ali Baba's house, he could not then kill him, since he would feel obliged to treat him well. But of course Ali Baba did not know the real reason why his guest did not wish to eat salt just then, and thought it was only because it did not agree with him. So without thinking any more about the matter, he went and told Morgiana to be sure not to put any salt in the supper she was getting ready, for his guest did not like it. Morgiana, however, was not so easily satisfied. As she was laying the dishes on the supper table, she took a good look at the strange guest who would not eat salt in her master's house. Although Cogia Houssain was so well disguised, she knew him at once to be the robber-captain, whose plan she had caused to fail before; seeing also that he had a dagger hidden inside his garments, she guessed that he meant to kill Ali Baba, and quickly thought of a way to prevent him a second time from doing this wicked deed.

When she had put all things on the table ready for supper, she left the three men to their feast; and without telling her master what she had discovered, she at once set off to carry out the plan she had made.

Morgiana was right in thinking that the robber-captain meant to kill her master; for since chance had brought him into Ali Baba's house sooner than he had expected, he made up his mind to destroy his enemy now that he was brought face to face with him. He was just thinking, when supper was over, how he would be able to do this without any danger to himself, when Morgiana entered the room again with some musicians.

Morgiana had dressed herself very prettily as a dancer, and round her waist she wore a silver girdle, into which she had thrust a scimitar; she had brought the musicians with her that she might dance before her master's guest.

As soon as Ali Baba saw Morgiana, he was pleased, and called upon her to amuse them with her dancing; but the robber-captain was not so pleased, for he saw that he would now have to wait a longer time before he could carry out his evil plan.

However, he pretended to be pleased, and so the dance began, the musicians playing a lively tune.

Now Morgiana was a very good dancer, and had often won great praise from her master's guests by her graceful movements; but never had she danced so well as she did on this night. Her last dance was best of all; for, drawing a scimitar from her girdle, she held it high over her head, and went through many wild and strange movements; but just as Ali Baba was admiring her skill more than he had ever done before, he saw her, to his horror, plunge the scimitar into the heart of Cogia Houssain, who fell over dead!

Very much shocked, Ali Baba demanded why she had thus killed the guest beneath his roof; and then Morgiana explained how she had discovered that Cogia Houssain was really the robber-captain, and pointed out the dagger which he had hidden beneath his garment.

When Ali Baba heard this and saw for himself that it was indeed the robber-captain who had been his guest, and that Morgiana had again saved his life, he felt more grateful than ever to her. He promised not only that she should be a free maiden, but also that she should be married to his son and so become a great lady.

Ali Baba's son was only too willing to make Morgiana his bride, for, besides being beautiful, he knew her to be brave, good, and clever; so a few days later they were married, and a grand feast was held in their honor.

And now Ali Baba had the secret of the robbers' treasure cave all to himself and his family. Since the secret was most carefully kept, he lived a rich man for the rest of his life. As for his son and the beautiful Morgiana, they grew to love each other so well that it would not have been possible to find a happier pair in all the world.

## Abou Hassan
## or The Caliph's Jest

DURING THE REIGN OF THE GREAT CALIPH
Haroun Alraschid, who had conquered and
made himself ruler over all the countries of
the East, there lived in Bagdad, the chief city
of Persia, a very rich old merchant and his
wife with their only child, a boy named Abou
Hassan. The old merchant brought up his son
with great care, having him taught all that
it was right and useful for him to know; and
as Abou Hassan was clever, lively, and handsome, he grew up to be a very fine, pleasant
young man.

However, Abou Hassan had been brought
up so strictly by the old merchant that he
had enjoyed but few of the pleasures in which
young people usually delight; so when his
father died and left him the whole of his great
riches, he determined to make up for the time
which he had lost, and to enjoy himself now
that he had the means of doing so.

He first of all divided his riches into two
parts, and very wisely bought houses and
lands with the one half, deciding to lay by
all the money these would bring him in, which

would be enough to live upon in comfort, but the other half he made up his mind to spend on all those delightful pleasures which he had not been able hitherto to enjoy.

Having arranged all this, Abou Hassan next invited all the young men he knew to help him to spend his money. He soon gathered around him a large number of gay, careless companions, whose only thought was how to make the time pass pleasantly, and who were glad enough to take all he had to give. They met together every day to enjoy the splendid feasts given by Abou Hassan, which were always followed by delightful concerts, dances, and other entertainments, all of which cost great sums of money. They were not in the least concerned as to what would be the end of all this, and encouraging their young host in his wild pleasures, they took good care to get all they could out of him without doing harm to themselves.

For a short time Abou Hassan amused himself with these feasts and gaieties, and was very happy indeed; but at the end of a year he found that he could go on no longer in this way, since he had spent the whole of the money he had set by for such enjoyments. So he was obliged to tell his gay companions that he could not afford to give them any more feasts. He now quickly found out that they were no true friends, for instead of helping and comforting him in his trouble they forsook him altogether, and would have nothing more to do with him, since he could give them no further pleasures.

Abou Hassan was even more grieved by the unkind, selfish conduct of his former friends than by the loss of the money he had so foolishly spent on them, and in great trouble he went to his mother and told her of all that had happened. His mother tried to comfort him as best she could by saying that his friends were not worthy of the name, and she advised him not to despair, since he still had the other half of his father's fortune, which he had been wise enough to lay out in houses and land.

Her son replied that he was indeed glad he still had the means for them both to live in some comfort, and he would now know how to make better use of what he had left; but as he could not believe that his companions really meant to have nothing more to do with him, he said he would go to them each in turn, and, pretending to be in great want, ask their help, just to see if any of them were grateful for what he had done for them in the time of his wealth.

So next day Abou Hassan went to each of his friends in turn to ask their help, pretending to be much worse off than he really was, and promising that if they would lend him money for his present needs he would soon repay it; but of all those whom he had treated so well and who had helped him to waste his money, not one would now do anything for him; many of them even pretended not to know him at all.

Full of indignation, Abou Hassan returned home, making up his mind that since his gay companions had loved him only for his riches and not for himself, he would have nothing more to do with the young men of Bagdad, and would certainly never invite them to another feast as long as he lived.

So he now began to live in a very quiet and careful manner on the other half of his fortune, which was quite enough for his wants, and he kept to his plan of having nothing more to do with his former companions; but as he was lively, and fond of pleasant company, he made it a rule to invite one stranger each day to have supper with him. He would go to the edge of the city every evening and wait there until he saw some stranger who was about to enter in from the country. Then he would very politely wish the stranger good day, and invite him to have supper and spend the night with him. The stranger was usually glad to accept this invitation, and then Abou Hassan would take him to his house, where they would have supper and then amuse themselves until it was time for rest. Next morning, when the guest went away, he was told that his host did not wish to have any further dealings with him, since he had made it a rule only to entertain strangers, and not to make friends.

For some time Abou Hassan kept to this rule, and managed to amuse himself very well with the strangers whom he brought to his house; but at last his curious plan led to a very strange adventure.

One evening he was waiting as usual at the edge of the city for some stranger to come by. Seeing a very respectable looking merchant, followed by a great slave, about to enter Bagdad, he went up to him and very gracefully invited him to sup and spend the night at his house.

Now this stranger was really the great caliph, Haroun Alraschid, who had disguised himself so well that it was not possible to recognize him as the king, and who, loving such adventures, meant to enter the city as an ordinary merchant, in order to find out for himself if the people were contented with his rule, or if there were any complaints or plots afoot. He was very pleased with the looks of Abou Hassan, though surprised at his speech, and being curious to learn more about him, he very readily accepted his invitation and bade him lead the way.

So Abou Hassan took the pretended merchant and the big slave to his house, little dreaming that he was about to entertain the mighty caliph, Haroun Alraschid. When they arrived, his mother at once sent up a plain but well-served supper. When they had eaten as much as they wished, wax candles were lighted, and fruits and wines having been set before them, they prepared to spend a very merry evening.

Abou Hassan, being by nature lively and witty, told his guest, the pretended merchant, all kinds of amusing tales, and the caliph was so delighted with his host's merry talk and pleasant manners that he enjoyed his adventure more and more as the evening went on. He soon learnt from Abou Hassan the whole story of his false friends, and of the rule he had laid upon himself of only entertaining strangers, whom he expected to remain as strangers to him afterwards, and to whom he never spoke again. Presently he said that he should like to make some return to his host for the pleasant evening he had spent, and asked in what way he might serve him.

Abou Hassan replied that he wanted for nothing himself, and was quite contented with the present life he led, and that the only thing that troubled him in the least was the bad conduct of the *imam*, or chief priest, of the mosque near by. He said that this *imam*, with four old men who were his helpers, did much mischief in the neighborhood by not using the powers they had in a proper way, and by frightening and ill-treating all those who would not do exactly as they wished. In fact, instead of being a help and comfort to the people, they were a constant trouble to them. Abou Hassan ended up this story by saying that he wished he might be caliph for just one day, and then he would give orders for the *imam* and his bad companions to be well beaten with the bastinado on the soles of their feet, to teach them not to trouble their neighbors any more, nor to interfere with other people's business.

The pretended merchant said that it was not altogether out of his power to get the young man's wish carried out, since he knew the caliph well; and after a little more talk he suggested that they should now go to rest. Abou Hassan readily agreed; then the caliph, having thought of a merry plan, offered his host a last cup of wine, into which he had secretly put a sleeping powder.

Not having noticed what his guest had done, Abou Hassan took the cup and drank off the wine; but scarcely had he swallowed the last drop when the powder caused such a sudden drowsiness to come over him that he sank back at once into a deep sleep. The caliph now called out to his slave, who had been in waiting behind, and commanded him to take Abou Hassan upon his back and to follow him to the palace.

In this manner the caliph, followed by his slave, bearing the sleeping Abou Hassan upon his shoulders, left the house unnoticed, and passing through the city, at length arrived at the palace, which he entered by a side door in the same quiet way as he had come out earlier in the evening.

He quickly caused Abou Hassan, still sleeping heavily, to be undressed and placed in his own royal bed. Then sending for all the lords and ladies of the palace, he spoke to them thus: "I desire that all those who usually attend on me when I rise shall not fail in their attendance here tomorrow morning upon this man, whom you see asleep in my bed; and that each perform the same service to him upon his waking as is usually paid to me. I also wish that you give him the same attentions as you give to me, that you obey him in all his commands. Refuse him nothing for which he may ask, and let him not be contradicted in anything that he may say. Whenever it be proper to speak to, or to answer him, let him always be treated as the Commander of the Faithful. In short, I desire that no more attention be paid to me by anyone, while they are attending on him, than if he were really what I am, namely Caliph and Commander of the Faithful. Above all, let this joke be carried out in every little detail, not leaving out the most trifling thing."

The palace attendants, seeing that their royal master wished to enjoy a little joke on his own account, readily fell in with his plan, which they knew would cause them much amusement, and they all promised to carry out the wishes of the caliph to the very best of their powers.

The caliph, having thus arranged all his plans, went to rest in another room, well satisfied that his joke would be a merry one. He got up very early next morning, and just as the gaily dressed lords and ladies trooped into the royal sleeping chamber to attend the king when he awoke, as was their usual custom, he slipped behind the curtains of a little cupboard, from which he could see and hear all that passed.

As it was now just about daybreak, and nearly time for the caliph to prepare for morning prayers before sunrise, one of the lords came up to the royal bed and gently awakened Abou Hassan, speaking to him as though he were really the great caliph, Haroun Alraschid, in these words: "Commander of the Faithful, it is time for Your Majesty to rise for prayers."

Abou Hassan at once opened his eyes, and

to his great astonishment, found himself in a most magnificent sleeping chamber, decorated with fine paintings, the richest hangings of silk, and tall vases of gold and silver. The bed he lay upon had a handsome covering of cloth of gold, trimmed with pearls and diamonds, and close beside it lay a gorgeous royal robe and a caliph's turban, glittering with jewels. He saw that he was quite surrounded by a number of richly dressed lords and most beautiful ladies, many of them carrying musical instruments, and all of them apparently waiting for his commands.

Full of amazement, Abou Hassan rubbed his eyes, thinking that he must surely be dreaming; but when the lord nearest the bed again spoke to him as "Your Majesty," saying that he must certainly rise, or he would be late for early prayers, which he never missed, he started up in joy, feeling that perhaps he was awake after all, since he could hear someone speaking to him.

The beautiul young ladies of the palace now came forward and began a concert of sweet music, which pleased Abou Hassan so much that he lay back once more amongst his downy cushions and listened with his eyes closed; but, presently, Mesrour, the chief attendant, came forward and said:

"Commander of the Faithful, the hour of prayer is past, and it will soon be time for you to attend to the usual state affairs of the day. If Your Majesty has not had a bad night, I beg of you to rise, as your presence will be required in the throne room!"

Abou Hassan stared hard at Mesrour for a few moments and then said: "Why do you call me 'Commander of the Faithful,' and 'Your Majesty'? You are making a great mistake, for I do not even know you!"

Mesrour, however, assured the young man that he made no mistake, since he was his own faithful slave, who had loved and served him as caliph and king for many long years, adding:

"I fear Your Majesty must have been upset by some bad dream, or you would not speak so strangely!"

At this Abou Hassan lay back and laughed heartily, and then, being still full of wonder, he said to a little slave who stood close by: "Tell me who I am!"

"Your Majesty is the great caliph Haroun Alraschid, Commander of the Faithful!" replied the little boy solemnly.

"You are not telling me the truth, little one!" declared Abou Hassan. Then holding out his hand to one of the pretty ladies near him, he said: "Come hither, fair lady, and bite the end of my finger, that I may feel whether I am awake or asleep!"

The lady, who knew that the real caliph was watching this amusing scene and wished to please him still more, went up to Abou Hassan with a very serious face and bit the finger he held up so hard that he called out in pain, to the concealed merriment of all in the room.

"I find I am awake!" cried Abou Hassan, snatching his finger away, and adding to the lady who had bitten him: "Now tell me, do *you* say that I am the Commander of the Faithful?"

"Oh yes, Your Majesty," replied the lady, "and we, your slaves, wonder that you will not believe that it is so!"

Abou Hassan still could not understand how such a thing could be, but he made up his mind to rise and see what would happen next.

The attendants now rushed forward to help him to dress, and when they had clothed him in the dazzling royal robe and placed the caliph's turban on his head, Mesrour led him through the midst of the bowing lords and ladies to the throne room, where the affairs of state went forward. He was helped up to the throne, and when seated, all the guards, ministers, and lords gathered around set up a great shout of welcome, and wished him happiness and good fortune. The real caliph now came out from his first hiding place and went into a second recess, from which he might see and hear all that took place in the throne room.

Abou Hassan now felt that he really had become caliph in some wonderful way or other, and since he found himself in such a happy position, he made up his mind to act as became a king. So when Giafar, the grand vizier, came up to the throne to receive his commands, he told him to give orders that the usual affairs of state for the day should go forward at once. The doors were then thrown open, and a crowd of viziers, officers, and other important nobles, all richly dressed in their most gorgeous robes of state, came forward, and bowing low before the throne, paid their respects to Abou Hassan as the caliph. After this several state matters of little importance were gone through.

While all this was going on, Abou Hassan noticed that the judge of the police, whom he knew by sight, was in the room. Remembering his wish of the night before, he called him to the front of the throne. As soon as the judge came forward, he commanded him to go with his attendants to the mosque of which he had spoken to the real caliph, seize the bad *imam* and the four old men he would find there, and beat them well, giving the old men a hundred strokes each with the bastinado and the *imam* himself four hundred; after which he was to mount them all, dressed in rags, on asses, with their faces toward the tails, and lead them through the city with a crier going before them, who should call out:

"This is the punishment of all those who do mischief and interfere with other people's business!"

He also said that not one of the five men was to be allowed to have anything to do with the mosque afterward, or even to enter that part of the town again; and he ordered the judge to come back very soon to tell him if all had been done as he desired.

The caliph was delighted with the bold tone in which this punishment was commanded to be carried out; he was greatly amused at the kingly manner in which Abou Hassan now conducted himself, and also at the ease with which the whole court had entered into the frolic he had arranged.

After a while the judge of police returned, and bowing before the supposed caliph, said that His Majesty's command had been duly carried out, and that the wicked *imam* and his four companions were now being led round the city on asses, with a crier going before them.

Abou Hassan was very pleased that his first command had been so well carried out, and he thought he would now try another. He called the grand vizier up to the throne this time, and told him to give orders that a bag containing a thousand pieces of gold should be sent at once to the mother of a certain young man named Abou Hassan, who lived in the part of the city to which the judge of police had just been sent. The grand vizier quickly left the room. Fetching a bag filled with a thousand pieces of gold, he ordered a slave to take it at once to Abou Hassan's mother and say to her: "The caliph makes you this present." The slave went directly to Abou Hassan's mother, who received the gift with the greatest surprise, for she had no idea why it had been sent. The grand vizier returned to the hall and told the pretended caliph that his command had been faithfully carried out.

At last the royal council came to an end, and Abou Hassan was led out of the throne room to pass the rest of the day in feasting and amusements, as was the real caliph's usual custom. He was now taken into a most magnificent hall, where a splendid feast was laid out for him in golden dishes. Here seven bands of music were playing all kinds of delightful tunes, and young ladies, dressed in most brilliant robes, came forward to fan him.

Abou Hassan was so charmed with these fair ladies that he would allow only one of them to fan him, and made the others sit down at table with him instead, that he might admire them a little more closely. He talked to them, and finding that they bore such names as Coral Lips, Heart's Delight, Moon Face, Sunshine, and so on, he made all kinds of merry jests about them, and said so many funny things that the caliph (who could still see and hear all that was going on) was beside himself with laughter, and was very pleased with the success of his joke.

After Abou Hassan had feasted at this table for some time, he was taken into another splendid room, where a rich dessert of the finest fruits was laid out in basins of pure gold. Here he found seven more grandly dressed ladies, even more beautiful than the others, standing ready to fan him. Full of delight, he invited these ladies also to sit down with him and help themselves to the fruits on the table. Again he amused himself and the hidden caliph with the merry remarks he made to them.

When the pretended king had eaten as much fruit as he liked, he was led into a third hall, still more splendid, where a table was set out with all kinds of dainty sweetmeats, and where he was received with music and by the same number of lovely ladies as before. After helping himself to some of the sweets, and making merry over the ladies' names, he was taken into still another great hall, which was even more magnificent than any of the others which he had seen.

Here he found a great many silver jugs of the richest beverages set out on a table, together with golden dishes of cakes and dried dainties usually served at the end of a feast; seven other ladies, even more wonderfully beautiful than any he had yet seen in the palace, stood about ready to wait upon him.

Abou Hassan was more delighted than ever. Upon learning from these dazzling ladies that they had such names as Cluster of Pearls, Morning Star, Daylight, and so forth, he used his merry wit to make prettier speeches to them than he had yet spoken. And while he talked and admired everything he saw, the ladies served him with sweets, and played soft music to him, so that his enjoyment was quite complete. He no longer had any doubt but that he was really king, and he was too full of joy at the happy prospect before him to trouble himself any more as to how it all came about.

But it was now getting late in the evening, and the caliph felt that it was time to end his little joke, which he had so thoroughly enjoyed; so, acting upon his orders, the beautiful lady called Cluster of Pearls went to a side table, and pouring out a glass of wine, put into it some of the same sort of powder the caliph had used the night before. Having done this, she brought the cup to Abou Hassan, and presenting it to him, asked if he would listen to a pretty new song she had made up that day and had never sung to anyone before.

The sham caliph took the cup, and said he would be delighted if so fair a lady would sing to him. So Cluster of Pearls took a lute and began to sing. Abou Hassan was so pleased with this song that he made her sing it over and over again. When she at last finished, he drank off the cup of wine she had given him. The sleeping powder began to work at once, and as Abou Hassan turned to thank and praise the lady for her song, he suddenly fell back among the cushions fast asleep.

The caliph now came forward from his hiding place, and ordered his attendants to take off the royal robes from Abou Hassan, and to dress him again in his own clothes. When this had been done, he told the very same slave as had brought the young man to the palace to carry him back to his home in the same manner.

The slave at once lifted the sleeping Abou Hassan onto his shoulders, and quickly took him through the city to his own house. Entering the door, which he found open, he laid him down on the sofa in the room from which he had brought him. When the slave returned to the palace and told his royal master that his orders had been carried out, the caliph was very pleased. Thinking that he had now sufficiently rewarded Abou Hassan for his kindness to himself, by granting him

113

his wish of being caliph for a day, and so giving him the opportunity to punish the bad *imam* and the attendants of the mosque, he went to bed well satisfied with what he had done, and feeling that he and his court had spent a most amusing day.

When Abou Hassan awoke next day it was quite late in the morning; and, rubbing his eyes, he called out sleepily: "Cluster of Pearls! Coral Lips! Moon Face! Where are you? Come hither!"

But finding that the beautiful ladies who had so eagerly waited upon him yesterday did not answer his call, he was greatly surprised, and called to them again so loudly and impatiently that his mother ran into the room, crying out: "What is the matter, my son?"

At these words, Abou Hassan, staring haughtily at her, said: "Good woman, who is it you call your son?"

"Why, *you* of course!" replied his mother, much surprised at such a question. "Are you not my son, Abou Hassan?"

"Certainly not!" cried Abou Hassan. "You do not speak the truth! I am not Abou Hassan, but the great caliph, Haroun Alraschid, Commander of the Faithful!"

His mother, thinking that her son had perhaps had a bad dream, which made him talk so wildly, now tried to quiet him by describing the punishment that had yesterday been given to the *imam* and the four old men of the mosque near by, hoping that this story would give a new turn to his thoughts. But Abou Hassan only declared that this more than ever proved him to be the caliph, since it was he himself who had given orders for the punishment to be carried out. He cried out so wildly that he was certainly the Commander of the Faithful that his mother became really frightened and feared that he had lost his wits. However, she tried to calm him once more by telling him of the one thousand pieces of gold the real caliph had sent her the day before; but this made Abou Hassan even wilder than ever. He declared that it was he himself who had sent the gold pieces to her, and that he knew he was the caliph and Commander of the Faithful. Because she refused to believe him and kept saying that he was her son, he flew into such a wild rage that, scarcely knowing what he did, he even began to beat her and knock her about.

The poor woman's cries soon caused the neighbors to come rushing in, and when they saw what the young man was about and heard him declare himself to be the caliph, and not Abou Hassan, they made up their minds that he had gone suddenly mad. Seizing hold of him, they bound him hand and foot, while two of their number went to fetch the keeper of the madhouse. As soon as the keeper arrived, he dragged Abou Hassan off to the madhouse, where he was kept locked up in a grated cell for three weeks. As the keeper was of a very harsh temper, he was so unkind as to beat the poor young man every day for declaring himself to be the Commander of the Faithful.

At first Abou Hassan, in spite of this bad treatment, clung to the idea that he was the caliph, for he remembered so well all the delightful things he had enjoyed in the palace, feeling that they could not have been only part of a dream; but after a while he began to think that if he were really the caliph he surely would not be shut up in a madhouse and treated so harshly, and at last he made up his mind that he was only Abou Hassan after all.

So when his mother next came to visit him, he told her that he now felt sure he could not be the caliph as he had supposed, but was certainly her own son, Abou Hassan; and he begged of her to forgive him for the bad way in which he had treated her in his first fit of rage. The mother was overjoyed to hear her son speak in this quiet manner and readily forgave him. The keeper, declaring that Abou Hassan was now in his right mind, allowed him to go home.

After he had rested a while, and got better from the bad treatment he had received in the madhouse, Abou Hassan began to live his old life again; and, soon growing tired of his own company, he made up his mind to invite a stranger to have supper with him every night as he had done before.

Now on the very first evening that Abou Hassan went to the edge of the city to look for a stranger to be his guest, it happened that the great caliph, Haroun Alraschid, again came past that way, in the disguise of a merchant, and followed by his great slave. Abou Hassan, still not knowing that he was the caliph, recognized the merchant at once; but having by this time made up his mind that all his misfortunes had been caused by this same merchant, who must have cast some enchantment upon him which had made him believe himself to be caliph, he decided to have nothing more to do with him, but let him pass by.

However, the disguised caliph recognized Abou Hassan. Wishing to amuse himself again with him, he went up to him at once, and greeted him as though he were an old friend; but Abou Hassan said he did not know him.

In much surprise, the caliph reminded Abou Hassan how he had invited him to supper only a few weeks ago, and must surely remember this. Then Abou Hassan said he certainly did remember that night, but only wished to forget it, as he felt the merchant had been the means of bringing him into great trouble by casting enchantment upon him.

The pretended merchant, on hearing this, now sat down beside Abou Hassan, and begged him to explain what he meant, and to tell him of all that had happened since the night he had supped with him. Abou Hassan, calmed by the stranger's kind tone, began to tell the story of how he had imagined himself to be the great caliph, and how, because of this, he had been shut up in a madhouse and treated very badly. He ended up by saying he could only account for all this by supposing that the merchant, whom he had invited to supper the very night it all began, had cast some sort of enchantment upon him.

Now the caliph was truly sorry to know that his little joke had brought such real trouble upon the young man who had amused him so well, and he quickly thought of a plan by means of which he might make up to him for what he had suffered, and at the same time amuse himself again; so he told Abou Hassan he was quite wrong in supposing he had cast enchantment over him, and that if only he would allow him to be his guest again that night, all should be well next day.

After a little more talk, Abou Hassan, who really liked the pretended merchant, at last agreed to his request, and led the way to his house. When they arrived there, his mother sent up a nice supper, and they both sat down to enjoy it. After they had eaten as much as they wished, wines and fruits were brought in, and the rest of the evening was passed in amusing talk. When, however, the hour grew late, the caliph managed, as before, to put a sleeping powder into a cup of wine, without being noticed by his host; and having handed this to Abou Hassan, he was pleased to see him drink it off.

Abou Hassan fell sound asleep at once. Then the big slave, at the caliph's command, lifted him up and carried him off to the palace. Here the sleeping man was again dressed in a caliph's robe and turban, and laid on a sofa in the fourth hall he had feasted in when last he came. The caliph, having told his lords and ladies to treat the stranger once more as king on the next day, went to rest, feeling satisfied with the plan he had thought of for making up to Abou Hassan for what he had suffered.

Next day, when Abou Hassan opened his eyes and found himself once again in a magnificent hall of the palace, surrounded by the same gay lords and beautiful ladies as had delighted him so much before, he was full of the greatest astonishment; and when he was again called "Your Majesty," and "Commander of the Faithful," and told that it was time for him to attend to the usual affairs of state for the day, he did not know what to think.

He rubbed his eyes very hard, and told the attendants that he did not know them, and that they were making a great mistake; but the lords and ladies only declared all the more that he was certainly their royal master, the caliph, and must not be surprised to find himself in the feasting hall instead of in bed, since he had fallen asleep so suddenly at the feast the night before, that, unwilling to awaken him, they had left him where he was.

Abou Hassan said he could not believe this, for he had been shut up in a madhouse since last he was in that hall; but as the attendants declared he must have been dreaming, since they knew him to be their caliph, he called to one of the lords and told him to bite his ear, that he might know whether he was awake or not. The lord bit his ear so hard that he cried out aloud, and at that moment bands of music began to play lively tunes, and all the lords and ladies started to sing, skip, and dance around Abou Hassan in the greatest glee.

Abou Hassan, finding that he was certainly awake, and in some wonderful way the king once more, was so delighted that he began to join in fun himself. Tearing off his royal robe and turban, he seized hold of the ladies' hands, and danced, sang, jumped, and cut such funny capers that the whole room rang with laughter. As for the caliph in his hiding place, he was so much amused at the merry antics of Abou Hassan that he laughed louder than anyone else; and when he at last found his voice, he came from behind the curtains, and cried: "Abou Hassan! Abou Hassan! Have you a mind to kill me with laughing?"

Directly the caliph's voice was heard, the music stopped, and everyone became silent at once, and Abou Hassan, turning to see where the voice came from, saw the caliph, whom he knew by sight, and now recognized in him the merchant whom he had twice invited to supper with him. But so far from being confused or alarmed, he entered into the joke at once. He merrily told the caliph he had no cause to complain of too much laughter, but that he himself was the one to grumble if anyone did so, since he had certainly had the worst of the joke.

The caliph, delighted to find that Abou Hassan bore him no ill will, quickly explained to him more fully how the whole affair had been carried out, and how sorry he was that what he had only meant to be a joke had brought such trouble upon him; now he declared that he meant to make amends for this, and asked the young man in what way he could serve him and make him happy.

Abou Hassan said he had already forgotten his past sufferings, and that the only wish he had was that he might be granted leave to visit the caliph sometimes, since it gave him such great happiness to be in his presence.

The caliph was more pleased than ever with Abou Hassan's modest request, and besides granting him leave to visit him at all times, he gave him a a handsome robe and a thousand pieces of gold. That he might enjoy his company more frequently, he invited the young man to live in the palace, and ordered rooms to be got ready for him at once.

Abou Hassan was quite willing to accept this invitation; after having gone home to tell his mother of his good fortune, he returned to live in the palace. Here he very quickly became the chief favorite of the caliph and his beautiful wife, the Princess Zobeide, no party of pleasure being considered complete unless Abou Hassan was there to make his merry speeches. As the story of his adventures soon spread all over the city, his former ungrateful companions would now have gladly called him friend.

After a while Abou Hassan became still more happy, for the Princess Zobeide, seeing that he had fallen in love with one of her most beautiful slaves, a lady named Nouzhatoul, gave him leave to marry her. A grand feast was held, and great rejoicings took place in honor of the marriage between Abou Hassan and Nouzhatoul, and the caliph and

Princess Zobeide gave them many handsome gifts, and enough money to live in the palace amid great comfort.

For some time Abou Hassan and his bride lived very happily indeed for they grew to love each other more and more, and as they were both fond of pleasure and merriment, held feasts and entertainments every day, never troubling their heads in the least about the expense of what gave them so much delight.

But after living in this careless manner for a while they suddenly came to the end of their money, and then, full of dismay, they began to wonder how they should get more to enable them to keep up their merry life in the palace.

Although the caliph had promised to provide for them, they did not like, after the splendid presents he had given them at their marriage, to ask him for money again so soon. Besides they felt that they had been careless and extravagant and feared that their royal master might be angry with them if they told him outright how quickly they had spent his gifts.

However, Abou Hassan, remembering how fond the caliph was of a good joke, quickly thought out a plan; and he told his wife to be troubled no longer, since they would soon get more money from their royal master and mistress by means of a merry trick they would play upon them both.

Nouzhatoul eagerly asked him to tell her of what he had thought, promising to help him in every way, and Abou Hassan then said:

"We will both pretend to die, and you will

see that the joke will bring us in some money, and please the caliph at the same time. I myself will first pretend to be dead, and you must lay me out in my sleeping chamber, as if ready to be buried. Then you must go weeping to the room of the Princess Zobeide, who will, of course, wish to know the cause of your grief. When you have told her, she is certain to have such pity for you that she will surely give you some money for my burial, and a rich piece of cloth to cover my body. When you come back, it will be your turn to pretend to be dead, and I will then go in great grief to the caliph, who, I do not doubt, will have pity and give me money and cloth also."

Nouzhatoul was delighted with the amusing plan her husband had thought of, and she said they would carry it out that day; so Abou Hassan laid himself down on the sheet she spread out on the floor of his sleeping chamber and allowed himself to be arranged as though ready to be buried, with a piece of fine muslin over his face.

Nouzhatoul then went weeping to the room of the Princess Zobeide, tearing her dress and hair, and crying out aloud, according to the usual custom of the people of the East when they are in trouble. The princess ran up to her at once and asked what was wrong and why she wept so much; then Nouzhatoul, throwing herself at the feet of her royal mistress in the wildest grief, sobbed out: "Alas, Abou Hassan, my dear husband, is no more!"

Nouzhatoul acted her part so well that Zobeide never for a moment thought that she

123

was only pretending, and being truly grieved to hear of the death of Abou Hassan, who had so often amused her, she did her best to comfort the poor widow. She told Nouzhatoul to weep no more, since she herself would take care of her again, and she gave her a hundred pieces of gold to pay for her husband's burial, and also a piece of rich silken cloth to cover his body. So Nouzhatoul now dried her tears, and after thanking the princess for her great kindness, she took the money and piece of cloth and returned to that part of the palace which had been her home since her marriage.

When Abou Hassan heard how well his plan had succeeded so far, he was quite delighted, and told his wife to lie down in his place. He would now go to the caliph, and, playing the same trick upon him, see if he could meet with the same success.

So Nouzhatoul lay down at once and pretended to be dead; and after covering her face over with the same piece of fine muslin he had just snatched from his own, he set off for the caliph's room.

Here he stood weeping and showing such signs of deep grief that the caliph soon noticed him, and asked what was the matter. On learning that his favorite wept for the loss of his beautiful wife, he was greatly shocked, and tried to comfort him to the best of his power.

Never dreaming that Abou Hassan was really only pretending, and knowing nothing of the extravagant way in which he had lived since his marriage, he gave him a hundred pieces of gold and a length of rich silk brocade, telling him to bury his wife in a handsome manner and to use the cloth as a last covering for her dead body.

Abou Hassan fell on his knees and thanked the caliph, after which he took the gifts of his royal master and returned to his own room in the palace. Nouzhatoul sprang up in delight on seeing that her husband had also met with success, and they both laughed and rejoiced with one another over the trick they had played; but, on thinking the matter over, they found they would still have to act with great care, and keep up the joke a little longer, if they wished it to end as well as it had begun.

In the meantime, the caliph went to the princess' room to tell her the sad news of Nouzhatoul's death, and finding her sitting upon a sofa weeping, he begged of her to tell him the cause of her grief. Upon learning that she wept for the death of Abou Hassan he was greatly surprised, and he said: "Surely Abou Hassan cannot be dead, when he has only just been to tell me of the death of Nouzhatoul!"

"What do you say?" cried Zobeide, surprised in her turn. "Nouzhatoul dead! That surely cannot be, for she came here only a short time ago to tell me of the death of Abou Hassan!"

Upon this a great squabble took place between the caliph and his wife, the one declaring that it was Nouzhatoul, and the other that it was Abou Hassan who had died. At last, after both had sent messengers to inquire, who only made matters worse by quarreling on their return, for each brought back a different tale, they made up their minds to go to Abou Hassan's room and find out the truth for themselves. The caliph agreed to give Zobeide one of his most beautiful pleasure gardens if she should prove to be right and they found that it was Abou Hassan who lay dead in his room. The princess said she would give her husband a palace of fine paintings if his story were the correct one and it was Nouzhatoul who had died. Having arranged this they set out, followed by their attendants, for the rooms of Abou Hassan, which were in another part of the palace.

The two plotters soon learned of the approach of their royal master and mistress, and Nouzhatoul grew frightened; for though they had managed to keep up their trick upon the two messengers, who had come separately, she did not know how they should act when the caliph and princess arrived together. But Abou Hassan told her not to be alarmed, for if they both lay down and pretended to be dead, she should see that all would yet go well. So Abou Hassan and Nouzhatoul quickly lay down side by side in the middle of the room, and, covering themselves over with the rich silken clothes they had just received, they both pretended to be dead when the caliph and Princess Zobeide entered with their attendants.

The royal pair stood silent for quite a long time, surprised, gazing with grief at the sad sight that met their eyes. At last Zobeide said: "Alas, they are both dead! Grief for the loss of her husband has killed dear Nouzhatoul also."

"Not so," said the caliph. "Pray remember it was Nouzhatoul who died first, and sorrow for her loss must have caused the death of my poor Abou Hassan. I was right, you see, and therefore have won the palace of paintings you promised me if such proved to be the case."

"No, no; you are *not* right!" cried Zobeide, getting angry again; "for I am sure it was Abou Hassan who died first, and therefore it is I who have won, and your pleasure garden must be mine."

And now the squabble began again, the caliph declaring that it was Nouzhatoul, and the princess that it was Abou Hassan, who had died first. At last, in order to put an end to the argument, the caliph called out: "I will give a thousand pieces of gold to anyone who can tell me which of these two died first!"

No sooner had he spoken these words than the voice of Abou Hassan answered from beneath the silken covering: "Commander of the Faithful, I died first! Give me the thousand pieces of gold!"

At the same moment Abou Hassan and Nouzhatoul both sprang up, and, throwing the silk covering from off their shoulders, they knelt at the feet of their royal master and mistress.

Zobeide shrieked in surprise, but the caliph, entering at once into the merry trick that had been played upon him, began to laugh as though he would never stop, and cried out: "What! Abou Hassan! Do you want to kill me a second time with laughing? What made you play such a trick as this?"

Abou Hassan, delighted that all was ending well, now told the whole reason why he and his wife had arranged the little joke, keeping back nothing. The caliph and Princess Zobeide were both so glad to find their favorites still alive and well, and so much amused at the funny trick the two had played, that they readily forgave them for the careless way in which they had spent their marriage money, and promised again that they would always provide for them. The caliph gave Abou Hassan the thousand pieces of gold he had just offered, and the princess gave the same sum to Nouzhatoul for joy at finding her still alive. The royal pair then returned to their own rooms, leaving Abou Hassan and Nouzhatoul rejoicing over their good fortune, and making up their minds to spend their money more carefully in future, in order to enjoy the pleasant life in the palace which they both loved so well.